THE SHANTER LEGACY

The Search for the Grey Mare's Tail

GARRY STEWART

TIPPERMUIR
· BOOKS LIMITED ·

The Shanter Legacy: The Search for the Grey Mare's Tail.
Copyright © 2021. All rights reserved.

The right of Garry Stewart to be identified as the author of the
Work has been asserted in accordance with the
Copyright, Designs & Patents Act 1988.

This first edition published and copyright 2021 by
Tippermuir Books Ltd, Perth, Scotland.
mail@tippermuirbooks.co.uk – www.tippermuirbooks.co.uk.

ISBN 978-1-913836-07-8 (*paperback*)

978-1-913836-10-8 (*eBook*)

A CIP catalogue record for this book is available from the British Library.

Editorial and Project coordination by Dr Paul S Philippou.

Cover design by Matthew Mackie.
Editorial support: Jean Hands, Iain Maloney and Steve Zajda.
Map by Rob Hands.

Text design, layout, and artwork by Bernard Chandler [graffik].
Text set in Adobe Garamond 10.5/14pt with Lumos titling.

Printed and bound by CPI Group (UK) Ltd, Croydon CR0 4YY.

For Jean and Buster

Acknowledgments

I would like to thank Dr Paul S Philippou of Tippermuir Books for placing his trust in my first novel. His support and expertise along with his dedicated colleagues at Tippermuir helped to make the journey enjoyable and fulfilling. I am indebted to Dr Pamela Carter for her support and advice through numerous re-writes and re-workings of the story. Thanks also to Sean Adams who inspired me with original art work for cover ideas. My appreciation also goes to the staff at the Coupar Institute Library where a large part of the book was written.

Thanks to David Goodall at Soundsmove for producing the trailer for the book. Finally, I want to thank my mum and dad, Jean and Buster, for giving me a wonderful childhood and two fantastic sisters; as well as my own children Callum and Eilean who are the embodiment of Fiona and Finn.

Chapter 1

THE NIGHT OF THE STORM

Fiona watched as the tail was ripped from the fleeing horse, leaving a terrible, bloody and gaping wound.

She sat up gasping for breath, her white knuckles gripping the bed covers. For seven nights in a row Fiona had been startled awake at the same point in this dreadful nightmare. She was trembling with fear and for a moment unsure of where she was. Breathing heavily, she took in her surroundings and was relieved to see her little brother Finn lying safely asleep in the bed beside her. Her breathing calmed slightly. She was glad that it was over, at least for tonight.

Slipping from under the covers she crossed to the window and peered out at the wild winter night. The storm was at its most ferocious. A light from the barn shone feebly in the darkness. She wrapped her shawl around her and tried to shrug off the unsettling images in her mind. Her thoughts turned to the day's work on the farm which had been long and hard. All day they had toiled to prepare for the onslaught of the storm. In the dark, the freezing icy gusts cut and lashed them as they battened down the last of the shutters and finally withdrew into the heart and hearth of the house, bone weary but happy in the knowledge that what needed to be done was done.

Kirsty had accompanied them for most of the day. As a border collie her main task was to make sure that both Finn and Fiona carried out their work in an effective and efficient manner. Alert eyes and ears set above a speckled nose showed an intelligence and determination that would put most farm labourers to shame. Fiona smiled for she loved the dog. She liked her life and living on the farm with her mother and little brother. Why then had she sensed that everything was going to change? She wished Finn would wake up so they could talk. She liked listening to him because he spoke such nonsense. He was only ten and she knew that when he grew up his nonsense would stop.

When the children had come up to bed Fiona had read Finn a story from the small chapbook their mother had bought them at the market and wondered if the mystical stories of elves, fauns and faeries had anything to do with the nightmares she'd been having. She shivered. Climbing back into bed she snuggled close to Finn to get some warmth. Finn stirred and murmured.

'You hold the giraffe's head. I'll give it the medicine.' Fiona snorted and giggled, even in his sleep Finn talked nonsense. She drifted off reminding herself to ask him what he had been dreaming about.

As dawn broke the freezing anger of the storm subsided into an arctic cold and moody dark morning. The snow lay deep upon the land, huge mounds and drifts covered the walls and outbuildings of the farm. The sky brooded with dark doom-laden clouds. The bare trees sat weary and twisted in the landscape.

As the cockerel crowed Kirsty raced from the fireside to wake the children. She barged into their room and, landing on the bed, aimed her first her collie-tongue-lick at Finn who was lying on his back in the middle of a huge yawn. Kirsty's tongue licked right inside his mouth and her wet nose poked him in the eye.

'Yuck!' yelled Finn trying to sweep the dog off the bed. Kirsty ducked under his arm. Her second lick was aimed at Finn's freckled cheek. Turning to avoid this, Finn got the dog's tongue in his ear along with a snort which practically deafened him.

Kirsty turned her attention to Fiona who had dived under the covers. Incensed at being outwitted, Kirsty yelped and tore at the cover, growling and jumping all over Finn in the process. Finn jack-knifed into a sitting position as Kirsty stomped on him.

'Ow!' he yelled.' The hairy mutt's stood on my wee man.'

Fiona fell off the bed laughing as their mother entered the room.

'What in the name of goodness is all this nonsense?' asked Kate. 'Kirsty! Come in by.'

Kirsty shot over and sat leaning obediently against Kate's leg.

'I've told you about getting this beast all excited. Now get yourselves dressed. The porridge is over the fire. Once we've had breakfast you'll have to check the animals in the barn and fix any damage that's been caused by the storm.' Kate turned and gently descended the stairs followed by Kirsty.

It was cold in the room and Fiona changed quickly behind the screen which gave her a small area of privacy. She sat on her stool brushing her long red hair, winding it into a bun and pinning it with the whalebone pin her father had carved for her.

'What were you dreaming about?' she asked Finn from behind the screen.

'Do you remember the other night I dreamt I had a pet gorilla?'

'How could I forget that?' laughed Fiona.

'Well, last night I dreamt I got bored with it because all it wanted to do was to pick nits out of my hair, so in the dream I swapped it for a giraffe.'

'It really is quite scary the things that go on in your head,' said Fiona, popping her head round the screen. Finn was still lying in bed. 'Finn get up and get dressed, we've got lots to do today!'

'I am dressed.' He started to pull his nightgown over his head to reveal his everyday clothes underneath. Fiona was horrified.

'Please don't tell me you slept with your clothes on.'

'I got the idea last night,' said Finn. 'It saved me lots of time this morning.'

'You are a clarty wee midden. Don't you dare do that again.'

'Why not? It saves time and I got to stay in bed a little bit longer.'

'I don't care,' argued Fiona. 'I have to share with you. I hope you washed before you put your nightgown on.'

'There's a daft idea too,' Finn argued back. 'What's the point of washing at night when you have to get up and do it again in the morning?'

'I'm not arguing with you, Finn. If you do it again I'll tell Mum and she'll give you a bath in the big tub in front of the fire.'

'All right, I'm only trying to be clever and find ways to save time!'

'Find ways to be a stinky wee grub, you mean. No wonder you dream about gorillas picking nits out of your hair. Now come on. We need to get breakfast.'

Over in the barn, Meg the grey mare stood silent and uneasy in her stall. She had been awake all through the storm, reliving the supernatural events that had maimed her fourteen years before. She quivered as the barn owl dropped from the rafters, spreading his wings before landing, breaking the back and nipping the neck of a scurrying mouse. He lifted off the floor and alighted on the stall in front of Meg's face, the mouse hanging from his beak as if it were merely sleeping. Pinning down his morsel he stripped a long piece from its warm, furry body. Blood seeped into the wooden spar of the stall.

In the corner of the shadowy barn, unseen and undetected by the creatures present, lurked the cloaked and hooded figure of a mysterious waiting man.

Chapter 2

31 OCTOBER 1804 — START OF THE STRANGEST DAY

Once downstairs, steaming bowls of porridge and cups of warm milk awaited the children. The fire blazed in the hearth as Finn's wooden spoon scraped the last morsel from his bowl. He always finished first.

'Mum,' he asked 'will you count my freckles later? I think I've got a new one.'

'I'll count them tonight at bedtime but I haven't noticed any new ones.'

'It's not fair. I hate having freckles.'

'Well, you shouldn't. Freckles are faerie kisses, kisses they only give to the bonniest of babies. They'll bring you luck.'

'You are just saying that to make me feel better.'

Fiona was waiting impatiently for the freckle talk to stop. She wanted to ask her mother something much more important.

'Mum, Tilly Tulloch's granny says this is the worst winter that anyone can remember.'

Fiona's statement was calculated to bring her mother out of herself. Kate had seemed preoccupied lately.

'Is that so?' Kate stirred the large pot over the fire without looking up.

'Aye, and she says it'll get worse. She was talking to big smiddy Jock and he said that the Earth would get as hard as iron, harder than the shoes he was putting on the minister's cuddy.'

Kate swung the pot around the griddle away from the direct heat of the fire and joined the children at the table. Smiling, she smoothed her apron and tucked a wayward strand of hair behind her ear.

'Granny Tulloch's imagination is famous in these parts. She never could put plain words to things.'

Fiona pressed on despite her mother's attempts to avoid the subject. 'She said there was weirdrie in the way the weather had turned.'

'If there's weirdrie in anything it's in Granny Tulloch's head,' said Finn. His interruption was intended to be humorous but it was too close to cheek for his mother to let it pass.

'Finn, if you can't speak well of your elders then it is best to say nothing at all.'

'I didn't mean anything by it mother, it was just a wee joke.' Finn loved practical jokes and sometimes his love of fun meant he carried things too far.

Fiona was angry that his attempt at humour had stopped her questioning her mother and blurted out, 'Granny Tulloch said the weirdrie in it was our father's fault. She said he spoiled the witches' dance.'

Kate's voice was firm as she held Fiona's gaze with determined hazel eyes. 'That's enough Fiona, we'll not have old wives clishmaclash at this table.'

But Fiona was not to be put off. She could tell from her mother's tone that she was on the right track. 'She said the weather had been dreadful on the seventh solstice and that the fourteenth would see the powers of the dark triumph over good. She said it was our father's fault.'

'That'll do, Fiona.'

'No, it will not do, Mother.' Fiona's anger and frustration had caused her to top her mother vocally and all three were stunned into silence. Finn sat gawping, looking from one to the other. He'd never heard Fiona speak like that to their mother.

Kate repeated herself quietly. 'I said that will do. Your father was a good man, Fiona. We'll not listen to superstitious rumours about him.'

'Mother, what's going on? Everything's different. You're different. The neighbours whisper when they see us in the town; the weather is scary. Something unnatural is happening and everyone thinks it's to do with us.'

Finn was not at all sure about what was going on. He'd not noticed anything unusual apart from the weather being exceptionally bad and Fiona being a bit odd. But she was a girl and an older sister at that. Girls were always behaving in odd ways. All the same, he was beginning to feel a bit uneasy.

'Is Fiona alright, Mum? Has she maybe banged her head? Should I get a poultice in case her brain melts through her ears?'

Rising from the table Kate crossed to the fire and gracefully lowered herself into the armchair. She motioned the children to come and sit on the floor at her feet. Fiona felt the excitement rise inside her. Her mother never sat at the fire after breakfast, there was always too much work to be done. They were always given a list of chores to be tackled right away. Even Finn realised that this day was already beginning to be very different from any he could remember.

The children settled on the warm hearthstone and listened eagerly.

'Fourteen years ago,' Kate began, 'when you were just a baby, Fiona, your father disturbed a coven of witches gathered at Alloway Kirkyard. When the witches spotted your father they chased after him. He rode Meg as fast as she could gallop but the witches caught up with them as he and Meg approached the bridge over the River Doon. You see, witches cannot cross running water. Just as your father raced across the keystone of the bridge one of the witches reached out and caught Meg by the tail ripping it clean off, leaving poor Meg badly wounded.'

'That's my nightmare,' Fiona knelt up gripping her mother's skirt. 'I dream it every night.'

'Your nightmare is real, Fiona.'

'But I never find out what happens next. I wake up just as the witch rips Meg's tail off. How does the nightmare end?'

'It hasn't ended, Fiona. The worst is still to come.'

'So where is Meg's tail now?' asked Finn.

'They say it was taken to a dark and evil land called Dracadonia where it was presented to a Druid queen, the beautiful but deadly Morbidea. A powerful and potent magic was bestowed upon the tail. Tonight, the night of the Samhain, Morbidea will absorb that magic and use it as the key to a mystical portal, the Yett of Abandoned Time, allowing her armies to flood through the portal wreaking vengeance and destruction upon our world.'

'Tonight?' gasped Finn, fear showing in his eyes. 'This will happen tonight?' Finn searched his mother's face for some kind of reassurance but Kate could only nod in response to his question as she stared into the crackling flames of the fire.

'Why do they want to attack our world? What have we ever done to them?' asked Fiona.

'Many thousands of years ago Morbidea's ancestors were part of the elite Druids who ruled the ancient Celtic world. They revered and worshipped Mother Nature. One however, by the name of Morrigan, turned her back on those beliefs and began to learn the secrets of a dark and evil magic. Her followers became known as the

Dark Druids. Mannan, the king of the Celts banished her and those who followed her to the underworld. Morrigan's descendants have searched for ways back, intent on erasing all history of the elite Druids, destroying their stone circles and sacred mounds, eradicating the land and people of their memory for ever. Morrigan is long dead but it is said her descendant, Morbidea, now has the power to open that portal and lead her armies in a war of revenge.'

'Can't anyone stop her?' Fiona asked. 'There must be a way.'

'Our world is about to change, my dears. We will have to survive as best we can.' Kate stood and smoothed her apron as Kirsty lifted her head in anticipation. 'Now we have work to do and we are far enough behind as it is. We'll talk again tonight. Don't worry. I have a plan that will keep you both safe.'

Chapter 3

THE STRANGER IN THE BARN

Fiona opened the cottage door and Kirsty shot out, bounding across the snow-covered yard. The muffled silence was broken only with the sound of Fiona and Finn's feet crunching down into the deep soft snow. A watching raven rasped a warning caw from the roof of the barn and flapped off across the fields, black against the white landscape.

'That was a scary story,' said Finn as he watched the raven soar into the distance.

Fiona said nothing; she was wrapped in her shawl and her thoughts. Finn made a snowball and threw it towards Kirsty. She jumped and caught it in her mouth causing it to disintegrate. Approaching the barn it appeared to have weathered the storm well.

There was no apparent damage although the snow had drifted and piled against the side that had taken the worst of the winds.

Fiona drew back the plank that secured the barn doors. They pulled hard to open it against the drifted snow, giving them enough room to slip through. Meg and the other animals turned their heads as they entered.

'One of us who isn't me will have to clean out the manure,' smirked Finn. Fiona forced a smile back at Finn as they set about their daily routine. Kirsty made a quick check of all the stalls sniffing as she went. Finn climbed up onto Meg's stall and gave the grey mare a scratch behind the ears.

'There you go, girl,' he said feeding her a carrot. Fiona picked up a pitchfork and began piling hay into the feeding troughs as Finn cleaned out the stalls, shovelling manure into a rough wooden barrow which he would eventually take to the compost heap. Fiona was very quiet. Normally they would chat away as they tackled their daily jobs but today her mind was elsewhere.

'You're boring,' Finn mumbled as he sidled past with a pitchfork of manure.

'Shut up, Finn,' Fiona snapped.

'No, you shut up,' Finn fired back.

'I am shut up. I was shut up until you spoke.'

They both sat in silence for a moment.

'What are you thinking about?' Fiona sat on a milking stool with her back against the upright timber of Meg's stall.

'What do you think? I'm thinking about what Mum just told us.'

'I know,' said Finn. 'It's scary.'

Kirsty sat beside Fiona, laying her head on her lap.

'It's not just scary, Finn, it's terrifying. It could be the end of our world if they come here. They can't be allowed to get through the Yett. They have to be stopped.' Finn knelt beside Fiona and put his arm around the dog.

'Who could stop them? They are evil and dangerous. It would take a huge army to stop them.'

'An army would be no good. They have power enough to destroy a hundred armies.'

'Then we're done for.'

'There is one way they could be stopped. It is dangerous, but it is probably the only way.'

'How? What way?'

'We have to get the tail back before they can use it. We have to find that abandoned Yett.'

'Are you mad? Did you get kicked in the head by a donkey when I wasn't looking?'

'The problem is we don't know what the Yett looks like or how to get into Morbidea's realm.'

'Perhaps I can help you there,' a voice boomed from the shadows.

Kirsty growled. Fiona jumped and Finn gave a yell.

A tall figure stepped from the shadows. His blue-hooded cloak hung down to his ankles and a sword was belted at his side. His riding boots of well-worn black leather matched the saddlebags which he carried across his strong shoulders. The children were startled but the stranger's appearance and manner did not seem threatening.

'Sit, Kirsty,' he commanded in a pleasant tone. The dog obeyed. He stepped forward into the light and pulled back his hood revealing a young, intelligent face. Laying his saddlebags over the top spar of the stall, he gave the children a smile and a kindness of character showed in his pale green eyes. Finn moved closer to Fiona.

'Who are you, sir?' Fiona asked.

'That all depends. For now, call me Malcolm. I have come to help you. Tonight is the night of the Samhain and time is running out. Finn, fetch me a bucket of water.'

Finn took his sister's hand and started to pull her toward the door of the barn.

'Right you are, sir. Come on, Fiona let's get the nice man a bucket of water.' Finn thought to himself, this man is as mad as a bag of snakes. Malcolm looked straight at him.

'Snakes are not mad, Finn, especially when they are in a bag. The darkness soothes them. It is when you open the bag that they can become unpredictable. Now get the water.' Finn's mouth fell wide open. He backed off towards the door of the barn not believing that this mysterious man could have had heard his thoughts. Fiona had heard them too.

'Who are you? How did you know what Finn was thinking and how was I able to hear what he thought?'

'Because I allowed you to,' he said.

Finn returned with the water. He had thought of going to get his mother but his instinct told him better. He put the bucket in front of Malcolm and stepped back beside Fiona.

'You did right not to get your mother,' said Malcolm picking up the bucket.

'How did you. . . ?'

'No time for questions, Finn,' Malcolm interrupted him. 'There isn't a moment to lose.'

'Isn't there?' Finn asked.

'No! Not a moment. Six days to be precise. We need to borrow six days of time. Get me the candle from that lantern.'

There was only a stub of the thick candle left but Fiona took it out and handed it over. Malcolm held it between the fingers of his left hand and touched the wick with the index finger of his right. It burst into flame. The children looked at one another, Finn giving an incredulous smile. They turned once more towards Malcolm. He had cupped the candle in both hands and appeared to be moulding it into the shape of a ball. When he had finished, the wax was completely spherical, light emanating from it like a tiny moon. The children were transfixed. Malcolm extended his arm holding it aloft. He blew gently on the glowing orb withdrawing his hand, leaving the tiny moon hovering in the air.

'Wow!' Finn exclaimed.

Fiona circled the glowing orb looking at it intensely. She looked over at Malcolm, questions in her eyes.

'All in goodish time.' Picking up the bucket he launched the contents into the air and to their surprise the water floated and formed into a perfect liquid sphere. It hovered, the light from the tiny moon reflecting on the surface of the water.

'It's beautiful. What is it?' asked Fiona.

'It's magic for sure,' said Finn.

Malcolm took a small pouch from the saddlebags and poured a tiny mound of earth into the palm of his hand.

'It's not quite finished yet.' In response to a flick of his hand the watery sphere began to revolve anticlockwise. Malcolm threw the earth and as it touched the sphere it was absorbed into the swirling water creating five recognisable continents. 'You asked what it was. It is your planet Earth and the Moon.'

The children looked in awe as the world turned and the Moon shone onto its surface. Finn stepped closer to it.

'It's just like the globe the teacher's got on his desk, only this one is real.' Fiona too had a closer look. It was indeed real.

'What are you going to do with it?' she asked.

Malcolm was searching through his saddlebags once more.

'I am going to give you some borrowed time.'

He pulled out a small, brown leather book with gilt-edged pages. During this wizardry Fiona noticed that Meg was equally engrossed in the stranger and his creations. Malcolm opened the well-thumbed book. Holding it in his left hand he held out his right towards the levitating Moon and Earth. He began reading aloud in a strong resonant voice. To their amazement, the rotating Earth began to slow until it came to a clear stop.

Turn about and against thy grain
Turn once, turn twice and turn again.'

At this command the Earth began to revolve against its natural direction, followed closely by the Moon. Malcolm continued.

———

'For six long days
In seven ways
We'll widdershin the tides and waves
Solar shadows go and come
An' the Moon shall rise before the Sun
The Moon will rise an' the Sun will set
An' borrowed time is what we'll get
So think us hard on what we say
For it will surely come our way
Bringing in night before the day.'

By now the planet was rotating clockwise. The shadows in the barn halted, creeping slowly into reverse. With increased speed the barn darkened as the morning receded. The sun set in the east and night came upon them. The storm resumed and soon reached its climax before reversing its rage and becoming subdued by the approach of the previous morning.

The children saw flashing images of themselves and Kirsty going about their work. Eventually the snows departed as the Earth revolved in reverse. Three days passed, four, five. On the sixth revolution just as the sun was about to set, Malcolm bellowed.

'Return to your axis of former days
Travail in unnatural toil no more
For the time you have lent will cleanse you deep
Or feed the worm at the very core.'

The Earth and Moon imploded into invisibility and the barn fell silent. In the distance, the peel of a church bell could be heard.

'What's happened?' Finn's voice was shaky.

'He's turned back time,' Fiona replied. 'I think to last Sunday.' Fiona looked to Malcolm for confirmation. He was nowhere to be seen.

'He's gone, Fiona, he's just vanished. What has he done?'

Chapter 4

A TOUCH OF MAGIC

'If you don't know by now, boy, then you haven't the brains you were born with,' called a voice from behind. With a sharp intake of breath the children spun round.

Looming over the children was a distinguished but fearsome looking man. He wore a long mercury-grey coat. Silver embroidered edging traced its wide lapels and a blue-grey sash pulled the coat tight over a black tunic. Long white hair framed sharp angular features and flowed down across strong broad shoulders. His white neatly-trimmed beard highlighted a stern mouth and he held a long-carved staff in his ringed hand. He scowled at them with deep green eyes. He was a man who had little time for mortals.

'And what should we call you?' asked Fiona, fixing him with a stare.

The man looked at her sternly, assessing her spirit.

'You have a boldness girl, just like your fool of a father. And it will be your undoing if you do not possess the cleverness to go with it.'

Fiona's anger rose within her. She still missed her father very much. 'I'll thank you to keep your remarks about my father to yourself,' she replied tersely, struggling to control herself.

'Yes!' Finn added. 'It's got nothing to do with you.'

'Silence!' he roared. 'It has everything to do with me.'

Taking a deep breath, he blew towards Finn whose body was flung backwards and landed at the foot of a hay bale. When Finn stood up and looked down, he was shocked to see he now had four black paws. He tried to shout, but an angry 'miaow' came from his mouth. Kirsty, who hated cats, made a growling lunge towards him and a frantic chase ensued. Finn scrambled high up onto a stack of hay bales to get out of Kirsty's reach. He stood there with his back arched, his fur standing on end, hissing and spitting at the enraged dog.

'Let that be a lesson to you, boy. Think before you speak.' With a flick of his fingers the cat disappeared and Finn stood on two wobbly legs once more. It was hard to say who was more confused, Finn or the dog.

Fiona, still controlling her anger, looked at the stranger coldly. 'Is that the sort of cleverness you think I should possess?'

'Don't meddle with me, girl. You have no idea what you are dealing with here.'

'Maybe not, but I think I know exactly who I am dealing with, Master Widdershin.'

The stranger smiled for the first time. 'Clever girl, so you know who I am?'

Fiona helped Finn down from the hay bale. 'There's only one person I've heard of that takes pleasure transforming mortals into other creatures. Leachim Widdershin.'

'The wizard,' Finn gasped. 'What do you want with us? Just you go away. We don't want you here. Nobody wants you here.' A knot rose in Finn's stomach.

'Finn's right, we know all about you. You are not welcome here.'

The two children stood holding onto each other. Leachim laughed and walked forward until he was towering over them.

'You know nothing about me and although I may not be welcome, you are lucky that I am here. This quest you are determined to undertake will be doomed without my help. Even with it there is no guarantee that you will succeed.'

'So Malcolm is not the only one who can read our thoughts?' queried Fiona.

'What Malcolm sees I also see. We are one and the same.' Leachim crossed to an old barrel and seated himself, his hands folded around the rough staff and his elbows resting on his knees.

'If Malcolm and you are one and the same, why is it he seems pleasant while you prefer to be obnoxious?'

Leachim chuckled. 'I can see the parish school has not been wasted on you, girl. That is good, as you will need all of your wits about you. Malcolm is my opposing persona that I occasionally inhabit. As you say, he is rather an agreeable character. Now pay attention, both of you. There is much that you must learn.'

Fiona sat on an upturned box. She'd heard many things about this wizard. Leachim Widdershin was a renowned, well-respected, but rather unusual wizard. It was said he shunned the company of people, living alone in his castle with only spirits for servants. He was known for his disdain of mortals and it was said he often practised his magic on them for mischief and fun. Fiona did not fully trust him and what he had done to Finn was proof of his impatience. Finn picked up the wooden bucket, turned it upside down and sat beside his sister. He had no idea what was going on. He was only vaguely aware of the possibility of a journey that he did not want to go on, so he decided to leave the talking to Fiona.

'The story your mother told you is not exaggerated in any way,' Leachim began. 'Our main problem is that the timescale of events has moved on. Morbidea's armies are mobilising and the assault on this world is planned to begin in six days, on the night of the Samhain. What I need to ask you, Fiona, is what made you decide to take on this quest to retrieve the tail?'

'I suppose,' answered Fiona without hesitation, 'that I feel we are responsible. Our father's curiosity caused this to happen. I feel we have no choice. We should be the ones to try and fix it.'

Finn couldn't keep quiet any longer. 'What can we do? We're only children. We'll never be able to get it back.'

'Why are you doing this?' Fiona asked Leachim. 'Everybody knows you are no great lover of our world, so why would you want to help us?'

The wizard nodded. 'What you don't know is that the tail can only be retrieved by one of the same blood. Someone related to your father. There is only you and your brother that stand between Morbidea's armies and the invasion of your world.' Leachim laid his staff across his legs and pushed his shoulders back stretching his spine. Leaning forward he popped his pipe into his mouth. 'What you have heard of me are tales of fear and superstition. I have deliberately avoided the world and chosen a solitary and secluded life in which to study sorcery and the black arts.'

'Turning people into cats?' Finn said accusingly.

'That is nothing more than the easiest of tricks,' Leachim puffed his pipe, the smoke momentarily forming the shape of a cat before dissipating, 'a novelty I could teach you in five minutes. What I speak of is acquiring an understanding of the darkest secrets of the universe. To learn, comprehend and practise these secrets I must commune with forces that are not from this world.' His emerald eyes looked haunted. 'You see, you must know your enemy. In order to do battle you must take into your armoury all the weapons they possess and you must be prepared to use those weapons no matter the outcome.'

Leachim fell silent bowing his head, ancient memories causing his heart to ache. Fiona softened to him for the first time.

'Why can't you use those things you have learned to stop Morbidea and her forces?'

'These gifts,' he mocked, 'are not learned or mastered easily. They are acquired over millennia. Morbidea and her cohorts have been schooled and instructed by generations of the most accomplished masters. Despite being at a disadvantage, I will in time possess enough knowledge to oppose her. However, time is against us. If the Yett is opened from the other side, the powers I now possess will be of little use in stopping her. The Yett must be closed against them as it was intended to be. That can only be achieved with the return of the tail.'

'Have you ever passed through the Yett?' Fiona enquired.

'Indeed yes, the Yett has been my portal to their realm for many years. I have visited to spy upon them and acquire the secrets that will help defend this world against their aggression.'

'So you are part mortal yourself?'

Leachim was impressed that Fiona was clever enough to work out his secret. 'You are very bright. My mother was mortal. Her traits and frailties, although revered in your world, are a hindrance to me in my chosen path. I have, therefore, undertaken to eradicate them from my personality.'

'So Malcolm is your human persona?'

'Let's hope you will be as sharp when dealing with the trials ahead of you. That is, if you are resolved to go on this quest?'

'Yes, I am, and if you are going to help that can only be a good thing.'

Leachim nodded intently, 'I'm afraid you might find my help somewhat limited, but I will endeavour to do my best.'

Finn who had been silently toying with a stick blurted out, 'Just a minute! What about me? I don't want to go. Everything I've seen and heard is really scary. I'm only ten and Fiona's only fourteen. How could we ever fight all these bad things? If we go we'll never come back, we'll never see our mother again. Is that what you want Fiona?' He turned to Leachim. 'You're a wizard. Why can't you do it? You've got all the magic stuff. Why don't you go and turn them all into cats?'

'I'm sorry, Finn,' frowned Fiona. 'I'd made up my own mind without asking you. You don't have to come. I'll go alone and you stay here and help Mum with the farm.'

Leachim turned to Finn. 'You have every right to be afraid, Finn. No one will blame you if you do not go. It only needs one of you. As long as one of the blood undertakes this quest that is all that can be asked.'

Finn and Fiona looked at one another.

'I'm not letting her go on her own,' said Finn, throwing the stick at Fiona. She'll just get into trouble on her own.'

Fiona smiled and threw the stick back.

Kirsty leapt from nowhere and caught it in mid-air, halfway between them. She dropped it at Leachim's feet, backing off and waiting for him to throw it for her. Leachim threw the stick several feet into the air where it hovered teasingly. Bemused, Kirsty sat staring up at it, waiting for it to drop.

'That should keep her busy for a while,' observed Leachim. They laughed and for a moment the tension of the situation eased. 'Now, let me propose a plan of action. I will guide you, Kirsty and the rest of your group to the Yett and transport you safely through the portal.'

'The rest of our group.' interjected Fiona. 'What do you mean, the rest?'

From behind them, a woman's voice spoke gently through soft lips. 'He means me.'

The children swung round but there was no one there, only Meg standing in her stall.

'Me,' said Meg. 'He means me bairns, Meg.'

Finn shrieked and jumped up from his bucket. 'Meg!' he screamed, climbing the bars of the stall and jumping on the mare's back. He threw his arms round her neck. 'I always dreamt you could speak.'

'I know,' said Meg. 'I always did speak to you in your dreams. But thanks to Master Widdershin and the quest we must undertake, we shall be able to talk every day.'

Finn sat up on Meg's back and looked toward the wizard. 'Thank you, Leachim.'

Fiona went to Meg and laid her face against her long grey nose stroking her gently. 'Any more surprises?' she asked the wizard.

'Only me,' said Mouldy as he swooped from the rafters to alight on the spar.

'A talking houlet as well. This is going to be great fun,' Finn said delightedly. He had spent his life talking to animals but until now they had never spoken back to him except in his imagination and dreams of course.

'Let me introduce Mouldy,' continued Leachim. 'He can fly silently day and night. Mouldy will be our eye in the sky and will be a great advantage to us. Goodness knows we will need it.' Finn turned excitedly to Leachim. 'All you need to do now is cast a spell to make Kirsty talk.'

'Kirsty is a creature of action and a quick thinker. Have a listen and see what I mean.' He elevated his hand towards Kirsty who was still fixated on the levitating stick and she instantly gave voice to her thoughts.

'What's up with this stick? Why is it not falling? It should be falling.'

Leachim twitched his fingers and the stick dropped into a perfectly timed snapping mouth. Kirsty shook it and let it drop.

'Great catch, well done, first time too, who wants a turn to throw the stick? Wait a minute we're going somewhere, come on get together, bunch up you lot, where are we going? Get in with the group, what's that bird doing here? Come on we've got things to do, let's go, let's go everybody, keep together, that direction, no, not that one, this one, if I have to come round there, oh for goodness sake, keep together. Am I talking to myself, am I... ?'

Leachim raised his hand again and the dog fell silent.

'We wouldn't get a word in edgeways!' exclaimed Finn.

'I had no idea Kirsty had so much going through her mind,' laughed Fiona. 'Once we get through the portal, how will we even begin to find the tail?'

'We have one lead. Over the years the tail has been in their realm it has become a powerful symbol. We know it is kept in an ancient convent where it is guarded by a sect known as the Cadaveran Nuns.'

Finn interrupted abruptly, 'So all we have to do is steal the tail back from a bunch of old nuns?'

'Not quite, a Cadaveran is a creature resurrected from the dead bodies of women who were hanged in our world for murder. They have become undead warriors, led by their commander, Stinkeye Cadabra. They are fanatically loyal to Morbidea and for the last fourteen years have guarded and worshipped the tail. It has become a symbol fit for a sorceress queen and is soon to be delivered into Morbidea's hands. Stinkeye is the keeper of the tail.'

He pointed his staff towards the centre of the barn where a glowing image appeared. They saw Meg's tail set into a silver-tooled handle. The handle was at least twelve inches long, engraved and embossed with the most beautiful Celtic designs. Emanating from the top and billowing like sea urchins in a gentle tide were the grey strands of Meg's tail.

'This,' announced Leachim, 'is the object of your quest. This is what we must seek and find in order to save your world.'

There was silence in the barn. All eyes were on the tail and all thoughts on the enormity of the task ahead.

Chapter 5

THE GREY MARE'S TAIL

After gathering essential provisions for the journey the unlikely army was set to march off. Leachim informed them it would take many hours to reach Loch Skeen, near which the Yett was hidden. He would meet them there. In the meantime he had other things which required his attention.

Finn demanded that he be in charge of Meg which everyone was happy to agree to. He could hardly get into any bother leading Meg by the halter. Also being younger, if he got tired he could ride on her back. Two large sacks were hung over Meg's broad shoulders which contained bread, cheese, a large ham and a goodly supply of apples and potatoes. They also had oatmeal and a supply of ready-made bannocks. This food might have to last them some time as no one knew if they would be able to find any kind of sustenance once they travelled through the portal. Mouldy joked that if they had mice or similar rodents beyond the Yett then he would never starve.

At last the time came to depart.

'Fiona! We should say goodbye to Mum.' Leachim stepped forward putting a hand on Finn's shoulder.

'There is no need,' he said gently. 'Besides, your mother would not let you go. She knows the dangers you would face.'

'But she'll miss us,' Finn pleaded.

'No, she won't. For although you are going on this quest, you will also be here. Time in this world has been abandoned. As long as you return within six days, no one will know you have been away. They will only know of your journey if you choose to tell them. If you fail in your quest, it will be of no consequence for the Earth will be doomed to a darkness from which it will never recover. Now, we can delay no longer. We must be gone.'

Leachim pushed open the door of the barn. Kirsty was the first to dash through. Fiona came next, then Finn leading Meg by the halter. Leachim watched them leave, Mouldy sitting on his right shoulder.

'Look after them, my friend,' he said to the wise old bird. 'They will need all the help you can give them.' He put his hand up for Mouldy to step onto and held the bird aloft to assist in its take-off.

The previous Sunday, this very day they set out on their adventure, had been rather pleasant. It was mild and sunny for a late October day. Anyone observing the little group as they made their way through the fields and meadows would never have thought that they were in fact embarking on a dangerous quest. Kirsty shot ahead of the group, running here and there covering at least four or five times the distance the others were travelling. Finn skipped ahead sometimes throwing a stick or climbing an interesting bit of tree. Fiona was deep in thought. She was enjoying the sunshine and the smell of the flora. She marvelled at how beautiful the countryside was. Fiona listened to Meg clopping behind her and everything seemed to be right and in place. This was how the world should be: a boy playing, a dog running and nature making the sounds and smells of life. Her heart, however, was heavy. She knew that the very existence of these things depended on her, an ordinary teenage girl.

Mouldy had decided to conserve his energy and not fly too much until they were through the Yett. He sat comfortably on Meg's head which was the best place for them to have a conversation.

'Don't sink those claws in too sharply,' said Meg, her soft nostrils slightly flaring.

'I won't. As long as you don't make any sudden movements,' growled the owl.

They plodded on at a pleasant rhythmic pace, passing a village where the inhabitants now stood motionless reminding them that time as they knew it had been abandoned. This excited Finn.

'Fiona, because we've borrowed time from the past none of the villagers can see us, don't you think that's amazing?'

Fiona smiled. Finn had such a love of the world and the wonders of it. She knew that if they got through this, his experiences would make him a very special person.

'Look!' Finn was pointing to a plump, well-fed lad who was bent over a shilpit skelf of a boy, his fist clenched ready to punch him. 'That's Harry Beltcher. He's a real bully. Remember that day he called me freckle-face and pushed me into the duck pond?'

Finn ran over to Harry and looked straight into his paralysed twisted face. 'Hello, Harry, still picking on people? Think it's time to teach you a lesson.' Kneeling down Finn undid Harry's bootlaces and tied them tightly together. Turning over a boulder he found a fat worm and popped it into Harry's gaping mouth.

'Finn,' screeched Fiona, half shocked and half laughing. 'You can't do that.'

'I'm not finished yet,' giggled Finn. At that he took a run up to Harry and gave him a huge kick up the backside. Turning to Fiona he said, 'I wish I could be here to see what happens when time comes back.' They both laughed until tears ran down their faces.

Several hours later, without having stopped for a break, the group of adventurers passed through the small village of Moffatt and came to the edge of a wood at the mouth of a wide glen.

'We've made good time,' said Meg. 'We should stop here and rest a while.'

'A wise idea,' said the owl. 'Rest and eat. I will circle the area to ensure all is well.'

Mouldy took off silently, climbing swiftly into the sky. All the companions were glad of a break. Even Kirsty was happy to rest. Finn gave her some scraps of ham while the children ate bannocks and drank from a flask of milk. Meg munched on some chopped apples. Fiona had a horrible premonition that they were all experiencing their last moment of normality.

After their meal, feeling tired, they lay down to rest.

'How long will it take to get to Loch Skeen?' asked Finn as he stretched his sleepy bones.

'It shouldn't be too long,' yawned Fiona, 'maybe two more hours. Leachim said we should travel up through the glen until we find the path to the loch. I don't know how easy it will be to find it.'

'It should be easy enough,' said Finn. 'It's beside a large waterfall which should be easy to spot.'

'How do you know that?' Fiona raised herself onto one elbow and looked quizzically at Finn.

'Old Crusty Campbell, the teacher, told us about it in our geography lessons. He was born near Loch Skeen and he was always going on about it.' Finn stood up, picked up a stick from the ground and began an impression of Crusty Campbell. He pointed the stick at Fiona, rounded his shoulders and spoke in a crotchety squeaky voice. 'Sit up straight, you grubby little creatures, and pay attention.' Fiona laughed. Finn's impersonation was very good. 'Loch Skeen is the very beautiful place where I was born four hundred years ago, much nicer than the dung-heap you little stinkies live in. The water from the loch runs down the hanging valley where it forms one of the highest waterfalls in the land known as the Grey Mare's Tail. . . You, boy! Pay attention you little tyke. As I was saying. . .' Fiona didn't hear any more. She felt as though she had been hit by a thunderbolt. She pushed onto her knees and stood up, swaying from the shock of what she'd heard.

'What did you just say?'

'Pay attention you little tyke.'

'No, not that bit. What did you say the waterfall was called?'

'The Grey Mare's Tail,' replied Finn, his impersonation forgotten as he realised Fiona was onto something.

'You are a genius, Finn.' Fiona grabbed her shawl and hastily wrapped it around herself. Finn was taken aback as Fiona usually retorted by calling him a daft wee gowk.

At this point, Mouldy glided silently back into camp, landing on the stump of a tree.

'All clear,' he said. 'Leachim wants us to meet him further up the glen before sunset.'

'Come on,' shouted Fiona, 'let's get going.' She took the lead toward the main path up through the glen. Kirsty caught up and was soon well ahead of her. 'Come on, Finn, hurry up.' Finn ran towards Meg, springing off a log and onto her back.

'Come on, Meg, let's go.' Meg took off at speed. With Finn comfortably balanced they galloped together, the best of friends.

Mouldy found himself all alone sitting on his tree stump. Don't mind me, he thought. I'll just make my own way there. He sighed. Too much haste, he thought, as he surveyed the deserted rest area and all the provisions that had been left behind.

Chapter 6

AMBUSH AT LOCH SKEEN

It was early evening when they reached the burn leading to the Grey Mare's Tail and although it was still quite warm, cloud was forming and a light mist was beginning to roll down the hills.

The waterfall was visible from the floor of the glen and did indeed look like the long tail of a horse. It came from the top of the cliff in a narrow but incredibly powerful gush, rushing over the rocks and out into the abyss, spuming and cascading nearly two hundred feet to the deep pool below. It was magnificent. Fiona thought the water glistened in the evening sunlight with crystal clarity, that it had a magical quality, the distant deluge drawing her closer with the promise of disclosing a secret. She had no doubt the Yett was somewhere close by.

They continued along the narrowing path, moving in single file with Fiona in front, Finn behind and Meg bringing up the rear. Kirsty as usual scampered ahead then raced back as if rounding them up. The path rose in a gentle slope before splitting in two directions. They followed the one to the left over a bridge that crossed the burn. The waterfall could be seen between a cleft in the hills. The climb was steep, dipping in places so that they momentarily lost sight but not the sound of the waterfall.

As they climbed, the drop to their right fell dramatically away from the path. Any slip and a fall to the burn below would have serious consequences.

Looking ahead, Fiona thought she saw a fleeting shape disappear behind some rocks. She stopped as Finn and Meg caught up behind her.

'What is it Fiona?' Finn noticed she was urgently scanning the terrain ahead.

'I thought I saw something.'

'What?' asked Finn with a hint of panic in his voice. He noticed that further ahead Kirsty had stopped and was crouched in an alert posture. She was staring intently ahead and was perfectly still. Meg put her head between the two children and whispered.

'The dog's seen something too.' At that instant Kirsty gave a low gruff bark and charged off out of sight towards the waterfall.

'Come on,' cried Fiona, 'there's no turning back now.' She took off with Finn behind her.

Meg was finding it hard to navigate the path at any great speed, her four legs being more of a hindrance on the narrow path and her keen awareness of the sheer drop prompting caution.

'I don't think she's seen anything,' puffed Finn as he kept pace with Fiona. 'I think she's just spooked herself.' Fiona knew he was feeling scared and was trying to convince himself there was nothing to worry about.

As they came over the last rise the Grey Mare's Tail towered above them. It was mesmerising. A vast surge of water thundered down into the boiling pool at the foot of the cliffs. The noise was deafening and the spray from the water soaked into their clothes, the watery mist blurring their vision.

Kirsty was at the base of the cliffs running back and forth following a scent that seemed to disappear up into the rocks of the cliff face. The pool was about one hundred feet across and a path ran around both sides disappearing into caves behind the waterfall itself. The collie was barking up at the cliffs where strange shadows flitted between the rocks.

'What is it, girl?' called Finn as they came up beside the dog.

Kirsty looked up and barked again. As she did so, a large barrel-sized boulder hit the rocks just above them and bounced dangerously over their heads. The children looked on as another boulder came hurtling towards them.

'Look out!' yelled Fiona as she dived and pushed Finn under an overhanging rock.

The boulder hit the spot where they had been standing. They cowered under the overhang and Kirsty shot in beside them. Two more large rocks bounced off their shelter, one plunging deeply into the waters of the pool.

'Whoever's doing this is trying to kill us!' shouted Fiona. 'We should try and make it into the caves behind the waterfall. They won't be able to drop boulders on us in there.'

'We can't,' cried Finn pointing. 'There's something. . .' his voice was urgent but remarkably brave. From behind the curtain of the waterfall dark shapes moved towards them.

Instinctively he spun round to check the direction from which they had come. More shadows crept menacingly in the mist and this time it was clear their form was not human. Finn took a quick look up at the rocks and realised any hope of escaping in that direction was impossible. He turned to Fiona with a disbelieving look on his face.

'We're trapped, Fiona. Is it the Cadaverans?'

Fiona shot a glance across the frothing pool of water in the faint hope they might be able to swim for it. The story was the same. Dark inhuman forms swarmed along the edge of the water at the other side of the pool.

Finn gasped. 'Whatever they are, there are hundreds of them.'

They were completely surrounded and through the mist, on the very path they had just walked, shone the eyes of a devil. One by one the creatures appeared, their large heads set on small agile bodies with evil eyes glinting in the mirk. Fear gripped the children as more of the creatures began to materialise, armed with swords and spears.

Suddenly, the closest of the creatures waved a long-bladed sword high above its misshapen head giving a snorted cry, 'Kill them!'

Just as the creatures were about to charge, Meg burst among them. She galloped at great speed scattering them in all directions. One of the creatures hit the ground so hard that its sword went spinning, coming to rest in front of Fiona, who instinctively grabbed it and stood defensively in front of Finn. Meg was lashing out with her back legs, rearing and flaying with her front and using her weight to scatter the creatures in disarray. Some of them sprang up into the rocks, others, injured, limped off to get away from Meg's fury. No one should underestimate the power of an adrenalin-fuelled angry horse.

The sudden change in fortunes halted the advance of the creatures. Finn ran forward and picked up an abandoned spear. Fiona looked around quickly assessing the situation. Meg had completely scattered the forces coming from the direction of the path. She stood there snorting anger, the breath from her nostrils condensing in the air. Wild-eyed and alert, she was ready to attack once more if need be. Finn turned and faced the threat coming from the direction of the waterfall. They too had ceased their advance.

Suddenly a loud and strong cry came from above. 'Enough!'

They looked up to see three shapes leaping agilely down the cliff. Within seconds they landed nimbly in front of the children. Meg turned ready to attack once more but two of the figures had raised bows and were aiming lethal-looking barbed arrows at her neck. The third creature was unarmed and he looked intently at the children. Fiona pointed her sword and Finn tightened his grip on the spear. 'Put your weapons down and tell your cuddy to behave itself or my men will put a shaft through it.' Finn and Fiona looked at one another unsure of what to do. 'Do it, and you'll not be harmed. You have my word on that.' There was something in the tone of the deep commanding voice that told Fiona the creature could be trusted.

'Very well, but please don't shoot our horse.' Fiona threw the sword to the ground and glanced over to her brother. 'Put the spear down Finn.' Finn was unsure and shook his head. 'If you don't put it down they'll kill Meg.'

'Put it down, laddie, I promise no harm will come to you.' Finn threw the spear on the ground near enough to grab it again if he had to.

The sun was beginning to burn through the mist and a rainbow formed in the spray from the waterfall. A slight welcoming heat eased back into the remains of the day. The creature stepped forward out of the evaporating mist. The children drew a sharp breath and held tightly to one another; they were not dealing with devils.

What had appeared in the mist to look like huge heads were in fact large tightly curved horns on rather normal but goat-like faces. The beast before them stood upright on cloven hooves, its legs and body covered with rough fur but its arms were definitely human. It wore a plaid woven from a coarse fabric. Finn stared in disbelief. He remembered seeing a creature like this somewhere before. He recalled a drawing in a book about Greek mythology at school, a drawing of a creature that was half man and half beast.

Finn's mythological creature glared at them.

'Lower your bows,' he commanded. 'Let the cuddy come forward.' Turning, he addressed the hordes that had ventured from the caves. 'I want whoever's responsible for this. Now get about your business or I'll have your hides.' Immediately the crowds dispersed and disappeared back into the caves behind the tumbling water. The goat-creature stooped and picked up the sword that lay next to Finn. He looked at the familiar weapon.

'Wattie! Tam!' Obediently two creatures ran up to his side. 'This is Callum's sword. If he hasn't come to me of his ain free will by sunset, then clap him in irons and bring him before me.'

'Aye, chief!'

'And find out who else was in this stramash with him.' The two nodded dutifully and went off taking the sword with them.

'I am Sir William Murray, laird of Glen Skeen. You'll accept my apologies for your treatment.' It was a statement, not a question or a request. You are my guests now and as such are under my protection.' Sir William knelt down and extended his hand towards Kirsty. 'Hello there, doggy, and what might your name be?' Kirsty sniffed his fingers and her tail wagged slightly. Finn gave Fiona a quizzical look. Normally Kirsty hated goats.

'Her name is Kirsty, sir,' acknowledged Fiona, 'and this is Meg.'

'So you are the one that started all this nonsense, the cuddy without a tail.'

'Nonsense indeed, that's rich coming from a talking goat,' said Meg.

'Despite my appearance, I am human, so watch what you say, cuddy.'

'You've been expecting us?' questioned Meg.

'There have been rumours that folk would come seeking the Yett and here you are. But you are wet through. Come and we'll get you dry and fed. Explanations sound better with dry clothes and a bowl o' broth in front of you.'

Sir William led them along the path and behind the waterfall where, hidden from view, was a large rocky entrance to a cavernous complex of caves leading deep into the mountainside. As they journeyed through this labyrinth, the children noticed that many homely touches had been made within these caves. Numerous little dwellings had been created from cloth and wooden frames. Fires burned in most of these little homes and the smell from cooking pots gave a warm and welcoming atmosphere, very different from the threat they had felt outside.

'Their cooking smells great. I'm starving after all that excitement.'

'We'll get you fed shortly, lad. Some bread and beef broth will sort you out.'

Torches lit the walls of the cave giving a soft gentle light and, apart from the entrance where the waterfall plunged to the pool, the ground was warm and dry. The goat-people and their children peered from their dwellings as the group passed by and much whispering could be heard.

Fiona overheard a goat-child bleat out, 'They look like we used to look.'

Eventually they reached a tall stockade built from heavy well-constructed logs.

'My headquarters,' Sir William pronounced.

Two of his men stood guard at the entrance while others could be seen patrolling along the top of the stockade. Passing by the guards, they found themselves in a wide courtyard around which many work areas had been erected. Timber frames with rough cloth and leather hide separated the workshops from one another. There was the industrious sound of blacksmiths' hammers ringing on anvils. Flames fanned by bellows sent sparks dancing as various weapons and armour were fashioned and shaped. There was a mess area where some of his soldiers were eating and drinking. There was another workshop where cloth was being spun and leather tooled and shaped into belts, jackets and arrow pouches. Fiona strode along beside Sir William.

'Are you expecting a war?'

Sir William stopped. 'We are already at war, lassie.'

A smallish goat-man rushed up and saluted. 'What are your orders laird?'

'Take this cuddy to the stables, tell the grooms to dry her and brush her down. Make sure she gets plenty oats and water.'

'Ah'll not say no to a rub down,' said Meg. 'It's been a long day. Thank you, laird.'

'We'll give you a set of new iron shoes as well. Ye may be in need of them.' Meg was led off to the stables happily contemplating the comfort offered.

At the far side of the courtyard, hewn into the rock were steps which led up to a set of sturdy oaken doors. The large steel-studded hinges creaked as guards pushed the doors apart giving the children access to a wide, spacious room. A long wooden table lay down the centre with smooth benches running down each side and a carved oak chair stood majestically positioned at its head. Sir William occupied this seat. Fiona reckoned that at least twenty people could be seated comfortably at this table. A fireplace in the wall opposite the doors roared effectively, with the flames warming and helping to light the windowless room. Wall torches added to the light as well as the candles hanging in two cast-iron candelabra above the table. Kirsty lay down in front of the fire and it wasn't long before steam was rising from her wet coat. Finn knelt beside her.

'This is great,' he said, holding his hands to the warming flames. 'I'm as cold as a baldy chicken.'

Sir William gave a strange snort which by his expression, Fiona took to be a laugh or guffaw. She slipped onto the end of the bench closest to Sir William's chair.

'Thank you for protecting us from the other...' She stopped not knowing how to describe the attackers without offending their host.

'The other goats,' Sir William offered.

Fiona nodded. 'Thank you,' she said once more.

'I will explain all in time. But first you must change or you will surely catch a bad cold. I have a son and daughter who are older than you and your brother, but we still have some of their clothes from when they were your age. I'm sure we can find something to fit you both.'

A mournful voice emanated from the shadows of the room.

'You're back, laird. I didn't know we had guests.'

'What have ah told you about skulking in the shadows, Dan?

Always trying to hear things that are not for your lugs.'

An emaciated old goat-man emerged from a corner of the room. He leaned heavily on a staff and seemed to have difficulty walking. His eyes were cloudy and crusted with matter and his coat was sparse with hairy tufts sticking up all over it. He was the scabbiest, unhealthiest specimen that the children had so far seen.

'It beats me that you didn't hear me coming. Nobody can walk quietly on these devil's feet.'

'Dan, this is Fiona and Finn. Take them to the guests' quarters and get the maids to bring them some of my bairns' old clothes. Have them back here in an hour.'

'Whatever you say, laird. This way if you please.'

Dan ushered the children through a door at the side of the fireplace and down a corridor. He hobbled along, his staff and hooves making an odd clacking rhythm. Finn took Fiona's hand and squeezed it. She saw the impish grin on Finn's face as he flicked his eyes towards the old goat. Finn started to hobble imitating old Dan's gait. Fiona had to stifle a laugh and she squeezed Finn's hand even harder to make him stop.

Dan left them in a small bedchamber. It had a log fire and was sparsely decorated with a carved double bed and two wooden-backed, threadbare chairs. It was, however, warm and cosy. Shortly after, two maids appeared with a chest full of clothing and started to spread garments on the bed for the children to choose from. They worked in silence, glancing occasionally at Fiona and Finn. They looked somewhat more human than the males of their clan. Their dresses were full length so covered their bodies and human hands protruded from the sleeves. When they had finished they curtsied to Fiona who followed them towards the door. One of the maids turned suddenly.

'Have you come to save us?' she asked.

'I don't know what you mean,' Fiona replied.

'There's a rumour. . .'

The door was suddenly pushed open and Dan stood there with his staff.

'Get on with your work, girl, and don't be pestering the guests.' The maids scuttled off as Dan watched them go.

'It's best if you do not talk to the servants.' With that he closed the door and the children heard him clacking down the corridor.

'This bed is really comfy.' Finn stretched in all directions making a star of his body. 'It's huge and really soft. I've never seen a bed like it. The laird must be really rich.'

'That servant, Dan, is a strange one,' said Fiona.

'Of course he's strange, he's half goat! Everybody's strange here,' said Finn jumping on the bed. 'Come and try this.'

'That girl asked if we were here to save her.'

'She's not a girl, she's a goat-girl.'

'That's the point. They were more girl than they were goat.'

'If you say so but I wouldn't want to marry one,' puffed Finn as he landed on his back out of breath.

Fiona started to look through the clothes that had been put out for her. It was obvious that the laird was rich for the clothes were very fine and nicer than anything she had ever worn. She picked some dry linen undergarments and a dark blue woollen dress with white embroidery on the collar and cuffs and took them behind a screen to change. There were more fancy things to choose from but she was thinking practically of what lay ahead. When she came out from behind the screen she felt different, not just warm and clean. She felt the clothes made her stand differently, as though her posture had changed. She realised her hands were neatly folded in front of her and she quickly stuck them behind her back but that didn't feel right either. There was a dressing table with a mirror but she was afraid to look into it.

Finn was still lying on the bed making no attempt to get dressed. The comfy bed and heat from the fire had sent him to sleep. Fiona crossed to look at him. His face was dirty and his dark hair tousled. He looked like a street urchin. Fiona laughed and whispered so as not to wake him.

'If Mum could see you now, she'd put you in the bathtub and

scrub you 'til you screamed.'

Looking across she saw her reflection in the mirror. Crossing round the bed to the dressing table she slowly sat in front of it, looking deeply into the glass. What had she done? Why had she brought her little brother on this mission? What if they never saw their mother again? Shaking these thoughts from her mind she began to brush her hair and with every stroke she felt different. When she had finished she almost did not recognise herself. Pushing the chair back she stood and turned. The rustle of the dress was wrong too. She didn't make that kind of noise when she moved about a room. She clenched her hands together and brought them to her chin saying aloud,

'I'll ask the laird to have my own clothes cleaned and give these back.'

'What did you say?' Finn sat up, rubbing his eyes. 'I fell asleep and had a funny dream. Wow! Fiona! What's happened to you?'

'Nothing, what do you mean?'

'You're different. You look like a grown-up rich lady.'

'No, I don't.'

'Yes, you do. I've seen rich ladies at church and that's what they look like.'

'It's just a dress. Now pick some clothes and put them on. Go on, quickly. We have to see the laird soon.'

'I don't know what to wear. Help me pick stuff.'

Fiona picked out some clothes for Finn, thinking of the practical aspects of the journey ahead of them.

'Go behind the screen and try these on, they should fit you.'

'I hate getting dressed. And don't look.'

'Why should I want to look?'

'So you could tell people you'd seen my bahoukie and get me all embarrassed.'

'Don't be so childish. If I wanted to do that I could tell people I'd seen it without having to actually look at your stinky wee behind.'

'You wouldn't dare.'

'I will if you don't get a move on. Hurry up.'

Finn emerged from behind the screen and looked quite presentable. Although the clothes were of a better standard than he normally wore, the style was much the same. He was smartly dressed in boots, breeches, shirt and a waistcoat.

'Pretty good, eh? What do you think, Fiona?'

'You still look like an urchin. Come here 'til I brush your hair.'

'No way! It's not good for you to get your hair brushed, it can hurt your brain.'

'Rubbish! Who told you that?'

'Big Betty Broon. She says your hair grows out of your brain and through your head and if it gets pulled hard, or actually brushed, your brain will bleed you to death.'

'And you believe Big Betty Broon?'

'It's true. That's why she chases you with a brush if she gets annoyed with you.'

'What utter nonsense.'

'It's true Fiona.' Finn grabbed the brush from Fiona and started to waddle about the room pretending to be Betty brushing at people's hair. 'Betty's going to brush your brains out, brush your brains out. It's just as well she's big, she can't catch you.'

'You talk the biggest load of nonsense. Now come here. I promise to be careful.' Fiona sat Finn at the dressing table and began teasing out his tousled hair. They looked at each other in the glass of the mirror.

'Ouch! That hurt. Is there any bleeding?'

'No! And it wouldn't hurt so much if you brushed it every day.'

'Fiona, do you think he's built all these rooms inside the caves?' asked Finn.

'Yes, but I don't think they have always lived here. I wonder what it is he wants to explain to us. It's certainly a strange place.'

'I thought we'd had it when we were trapped earlier. Good old Meg sorted those goats out.'

'It was his own people who tried to kill us. We may not be safe even yet.'

'Well, at least the laird seems to be on our side and he's definitely the one in charge.'

'Yes. I think he's going to help us to find a way through the Yett. There! What do you think?' Fiona had finished Finn's hair which she had brushed into a neat side parting.

'It looks as though I haven't seen a gust of wind for a week.'

'I wouldn't worry. Your hair's got a life of its own. It'll be all over the place before there's a knock on the door.'

There was a knock on the door. Finn jumped beside Fiona.

'How did you do that?'

Fiona pulled the door open to reveal Dan standing in fine livery.

'The laird requests the pleasure of your company, if you will follow me.'

Chapter 7

THE CURSE OF THE CLAN

'Your guests, Sir William,' announced Dan. Fiona and Finn walked forward awkwardly, unused to being treated in such an important manner. The laird was briefly taken aback by the children.

'Goodness! I mean, welcome my young friends. I hope you are well rested.'

'Thank you, sir,' replied Fiona.

Sir William had changed from the rough clothes he had worn earlier. He stood before them dressed in a deep purple plaid held in place with a black leather belt displaying an ornate silver buckle. A silver clasp pinning the plaid to his left shoulder repeated the design. His white shirt sleeves billowed and on his wrist he wore a woven leather bracelet. A simple wedding ring was evident on his left hand.

He gestured to the children to take a seat.

The table had been laid with perfectly polished pewter plates and goblets. Fiona counted five places set for dinner. The laird stood in front of his chair and waited for Finn and Fiona to sit at either side of him before sitting himself.

'You must forgive me. I was a wee bit shocked seeing you dressed in my children's clothing. It reminded me of them at your age, which was some time ago.'

'Thank you for the loan of them. We will return the clothes as soon as our own are dry.'

'Nonsense, Fiona, I will have your own cleaned, dried and parcelled up for you. These however, you can keep. I no longer have need of them. You never know when you might get another soaking on this journey you are undertaking.'

'Are you going to help us to find the Yett?'

'Heavens, lassie, give our seats a minute to get warm, there's things to discuss first. Besides, as you can see, we are waiting for two other guests to join us.'

'Fiona's a girl, she does not like waiting, she likes things to get done right away,' said Finn who was beginning to feel quite comfortable in the laird's presence.

'That's no bad thing in some circumstances, lad. But in this case caution and a plan will not go amiss.'

'Who are we waiting for?' asked Fiona.

'Paul of the Lapping Loch. He's a poet, so he'll probably be late. The other person you will know.'

A voice boomed from across the room. 'And trust I hope.' Leachim was leaning against the fireplace smoking his pipe. No one had been aware of his presence or noticed him arrive. He tapped his pipe out in the hearth and crossed to the table.

The laird stood to greet him as did Fiona. Finn felt he'd better do the same. The laird and Leachim seemed to know each other well, Fiona immediately sensing respect and a bond between them.

'Are you hungry Leachim?' asked the laird as they all sat once more.

'I could eat a dead puddock,' quipped the wizard.

'I think we can do better than a deceased toad chuckled the laird. Dan, have the servants put everything on the table then make themselves scarce. We can help ourselves and we want to talk without being listened to.'

'You heard the laird, put the grub on the table and take the rest of the night off,' instructed Dan.

The servants speedily obeyed and departed leaving the table well supplied for the evening. The laird indicated for his guests to help themselves and it wasn't long before all the plates were loaded. Finn filled his goblet with a mouth-watering ruby red berry juice.

'Time is short,' Leachim boomed. 'We should talk as we eat.'

Finn looked at the assorted bowls of steaming chicken and beef. There was a mixture of aromatic vegetables glazed with herbs and soft, hot bread straight from the oven. The savoury aromas caused Finn's stomach to rumble.

'Someone who isn't me can do the talking. I'll listen and eat,' said Finn as he eagerly began to feast.

'You have certainly had an interesting start to your quest,' Leachim said, looking at Fiona. 'You really should not have been in any danger this side of the Yett. We underestimated certain circumstances.'

The laird poured himself a goblet of velvet red wine. 'That was in many ways my doing. You will have noticed there are divisions among my folk which are becoming' difficult to control. I will tell you briefly of our plight.'

The door into the room suddenly opened and a young, well-dressed goat-man hurried in. 'My apologies, laird, I lost track of the time. I hope your guests will forgive me.'

'I'm certain they will, Paul. Leachim you know. This is Fiona and Finn.'

Paul appeared a little awkward avoiding direct eye contact with the pair.

'Take a seat beside Fiona. I am just about to tell the story of our people. Paul here is our bard, a well-educated young man who keeps the history of the clan.'

Paul sat opposite Leachim, beside Fiona, quietly acknowledging the two children. The laird let him settle before continuing.

'Many years ago my people were human, just as you are. We farmed the land and lived simple and happy lives. There was, however, one great responsibility our clan had inherited. For thousands of years, we were the earthly keepers of the Yett of Abandoned Time, the ancient portal to the dark realm of the underworld. Our task was to prevent anyone from this world entering through the Yett, disturbing the forces that dwell beyond.'

'Excuse me, laird,' interrupted Fiona. 'You say you were the earthly keepers of the Yett. Does that mean there are unearthly keepers?'

'A good question. Yes, indeed there are,' answered Leachim. 'There is a race of beings who dwell directly on the other side of the Yett, tasked with preventing any from passing into our world.'

'In a sense they are our allies,' interjected the laird. 'You will have heard of the faerie people.' Finn almost choked.

'The faerie people: they steal babies from their mothers.'

'Aye, some have been known to do this,' replied Leachim quickly dismissing Finn's interruption. 'Carry on, laird.'

'For hundreds of years our alliance kept both realms separate and free from one another. We guarded the Yett, they on their side, we on ours.'

'Until the day she turned up,' growled Paul.

'Heather was not to blame,' snarled the laird. 'She became one of us and has been more loyal than some we could mention.'

'I say she was a spy, sent to beguile us,' snapped Paul.

'That matters little now,' said Leachim with authority. 'Finish the tale, laird, for we must plan and move on.'

Paul leaned on the table sullenly tearing at a chunk of thick cut bread. The laird sat back with his hands on the arms of the carved chair.

'One day a young woman arrived at our castle. She was lost and had been wandering for days through the hillsides. She could not remember her name or where she had come from. We took her in. Heather was the name we gave her. Her only possession was a baby's shawl which she clutched to her breast. Heather soon became a loyal friend and companion to my daughter, Eilean. We soon realised that she possessed great healing powers and an amazing knowledge of plants and herbal remedies.

As time passed her memory began to return. She told us she had been sent by the faerie people to steal a human child and leave a changeling in its place. The faerie child had died before the deed was done and Heather was banished to wander our Earth as a punishment. Eilean became enthralled by Heather's tales of the faerie world and of the magical realm in which she had dwelt.' The laird paused for a second, thinking back in time to when he had last seen his daughter, his grip on the chair tightened noticeably.

Fiona leaned forward and gently asked, 'Your daughter asked Heather to take her there, didn't she?'

The laird nodded despondently. Leachim smiled, he delighted in Fiona's natural intuition.

'She lured her there if you ask me,' fumed Paul. 'She had this planned all along. She took her from us.'

Leachim reached across the table and gripped Paul's wrist.

'I think you let your love for Eilean blind you to the truth of what happened. A poet should always keep an open mind.'

Paul pulled himself free of Leachim and jumped from the table. 'Love? No one can talk of love when you look like this. You cannot look upon beauty with any kind of love when you have the eyes of a demon. You cannot dance with beauty when you have the cloven feet of the devil. There can be no more love until we are free of this curse.'

Finn was finding all of this a bit embarrassing. Nobody he knew talked about love. It was a bit soppy. He knew he loved his mum, sister, Meg and Kirsty, but you didn't talk about it. He thought to himself, I'm sitting at a table with a love-sick goat.

'What happened to your daughter, laird?' Fiona's voice was soft and kind.

'She begged Heather to show her the faerie realm. Heather secretly arranged for the Yett to be opened by her cousin, Ostrand, who was a keeper of the Yett on the faerie side. Ostrand missed Heather very much and was glad of the chance to see her once more. He promised he would open the Yett but for three hours only, by the end of which the two girls must return.

'On the night they disappeared, Eilean's maid told me of their plan. Heather prepared a bath for Eilean. Into the water she poured tinctures of witch hazel and oils made from a blend of lady's mantle and sweet violet. A deep soak in this potion would bestow a sweet scent and a transparency emulating that of the inhabitants of the faerie world. She smeared a balm of gingko biloba on Eilean's eyelids in order that she might see more clearly in an otherwise translucent world. When all was ready they set off on their fateful visit.'

'What was unknown at the time,' interjected Leachim, 'was that her cousin Ostrand had shared his secret with a close friend who turned out to be one of Morbidea's trusted spies. He informed her of the plan to open the portal. Morbidea, knowing that secrets can never be kept for too long, speedily prepared an ambush that she herself would lead. She took command of a squadron of her Cadaveran nuns and deployed them close to the Yett.

'When Eilean and Heather passed through the Cadaverans struck. The girls were captured instantly and Ostrand was slain trying to protect them.'

'That was not the worst of it,' interrupted the laird. 'Morbidea realised she had the opportunity to pass through the Yett into our land for a brief time.'

'So Morbidea has already mounted an attack into our world?' Fiona asked.

'Not a full-blown attack. I suppose you would call it a skirmish,' Leachim answered. 'The consequences of that skirmish, however, have given Morbidea a great advantage.'

The laird got up from the table, continuing the story as he crossed to the fireplace, and lit a pipe. 'Morbidea led her squadron of Cadaverans through the portal and attacked my people. We were completely unprepared and although we fought fiercely they soon overpowered us. It was then she laid down the terms of our surrender. She was not ready for a full-scale attack on our world. She had to wait until the power of the mare's tail had been bestowed upon her. Only then would the Yett be open long enough for all of her forces to surge through. She also did not want her armies to be attacked by us as soon as they reached this side.'

'So what did she do?' asked Finn. Although the talk of fighting was scary, it was more interesting and less embarrassing than talking about love.

'She told us she would keep my daughter prisoner. If we opposed her in any way she would be given to the Cadaverans who would torture her in the most awful ways before killing her. In order that we would comply with her demands she cursed my people by casting a spell upon us. A spell that turned us into the fauns we are today. The beasts you now see before you.'

'I see,' said Fiona, 'so when she eventually comes to make war, she has promised to return you all to your human form if you do not oppose her.'

'I do not believe that she will reverse the spell she has put upon us, but many of my people do. It has caused great division among us.'

'At worst, some want to join with her in order to be rid of this curse,' said Paul with anger in his voice.

'Which is why you were attacked earlier today,' continued the laird blowing smoke from his pipe. 'I do know she has made a spy of someone in our clan. There is someone who warns her of our every plan.'

Finn who had just stuffed a large piece of chicken into his mouth mumbled, 'If there is a spy, how do we get through without Morbidea setting her nuns on us?' By the time he'd asked the question half of his chicken was back on the plate and a piece stuck to his upper lip.

'That's disgusting, Finn. Mum would choke you for that.'

'What? Leachim said we could talk and eat.'

'To answer your question, Finn,' said Leachim, 'your departure must be known by as few people as possible. But I think we can safely assume that Morbidea already knows you are here. She will be expecting you to attempt to pass within the next day or two.'

Fiona was slightly surprised by this. Two days seemed excessive considering the time pressures that were on them. She noticed Leachim watching her closely and was about to question him when he blew smoke from his pipe which formed the words 'Not now Fiona' in the air. Fiona stayed silent. A quick look at the others confirmed they had not seen the secret communication.

'Listen carefully,' continued Leachim. 'We will go early, the day after tomorrow. My gifts allow me to pass through the Yett undetected. I have done so many times. This time I will make sure that Morbidea and her acolytes know that I am there. I will create a diversion and lead them away from the Yett, allowing you to pass through quickly and begin your journey.'

'That's too dangerous, Leachim. What if they catch you?'

'They will not catch me. I have led them on many a merry dance in my time. It will take more than a squadron of Cadaverans to outwit me. We will leave one hour before dawn and cross through as the sun rises. When I have led them away you must both ride Meg as if your lives depended on it. Kirsty and Mouldy will have no trouble keeping up.'

'I have a two-seated saddle,' said the laird, 'with two sets of stirrups which will help you travel faster and make it more comfortable for the horse.'

'How far behind will you be?' interrupted Finn.

'Don't you worry,' Leachim chuckled heartily. 'I will not be far behind and we'll soon leave them chasing their own tails.' Leachim seemed quite amused with himself and Finn and Fiona smiled at one another wondering what he had up that wizard's sleeve of his.

Leachim stood. 'I'll join you in a pipe, laird. Remember, nothing we have spoken of goes beyond this room.' Leachim and the laird puffed at their pipes and spoke quietly together by the fire while Fiona and Finn mused over the events of the day.

Paul sat quietly at the table lost in his own thoughts. There was a loud knock on the door.

Dan entered. 'laird, Tam and Wattie are here. They have Callum and two of the perpetrators.'

'Bring them in, Dan.' There was a lot of scuttling and shuffling as Wattie and Tam pushed the prisoners into the hall. They were roped together and, although dishevelled, appeared arrogant and defiant. Tam and Wattie lined them up in front of the laird as Leachim slipped away from the fireplace to join the children. The laird stood looking into the fire with his back to the prisoners. He spoke without turning. 'You disobeyed my orders, Callum.'

'Aye. Orders that don't take into account the needs of our clan.'

The laird spun round furiously and the arrogance of the prisoners faltered slightly.

'I am clan chief, I'll decide how the needs of the clan are met!' he bellowed. 'You and your ruffians attacked these bairns and would have killed them if their cuddy hadn't saved them. Do you want their blood on your hands?'

'If it frees us from the spell then aye,' shot back Callum. 'It's all right for you. You and all the others who make the decisions, you're old. We're young, we don't want to spend our life like this. If we give Morbidea what she wants she'll free us from the spell.'

'Give her what she wants? Have you any idea what you're saying? Morbidea is never going to free us from this curse. She has us where she wants us. Our only chance is to stay united and fight her as best we can. If we are not united then we are doomed.'

'We're doomed anyway,' Callum retorted. 'We can never defeat her.'

'I didn't say we could defeat her, I said we could fight her. And we can die trying to defeat her.'

Callum straightened up and looked the laird in the eyes. 'We are not afraid to fight and die. But not like this. We'll fight and die like honest folk.'

The laird looked at him sadly, rebuking in a softer manner. 'And what kind of person would you be if you had the blood of these two bairns on your hands? You three led a clan revolt. Now you'll pay the price. You'll be tried by a council of elders and if you are found guilty. . . you'll hang.'

There was silence at the laird's pronouncement; the prisoners exchanged solemn glances with each other. Even Wattie and Tam seemed shaken by the proclamation.

'You leave me no choice. Take them to the dungeon, Wattie.'

Tam and Wattie led the three prisoners towards the door and as it closed behind them the laird, looking very tired, slumped into his chair.

'You can't be serious, laird. We have never tried and executed any of our own folk in the entire history of the clan.'

'Then you had better sharpen your quills, Paul, for it looks as if a new chapter of our history is about to be written.'

Later that evening when the children returned to their bedchamber, they sat on the inviting bed and talked quietly about the events of the day. The fire crackled in the grate as shadows flickered and danced on the high walls and ceiling. Eventually, exhausted, they fell asleep on top of the coverlet as the evening outside darkened.

Chapter 8

MORBIDEA'S SPY

In the dank, dark of the evening, on the other side of the Yett, a cloaked and hooded figure crept stealthily to where Morbidea's squadron was encamped. Keeping to the shadows, he silently avoided the campfires that might warn the Cadaverans of his approach.

The hooded figure knew these creatures well, for he was Morbidea's spy. He had witnessed them in action, their vicious and ferocious atrocities horrifying him. They were her most trusted troops, every one of them a resurrected cadaver of a murderess. Cut from the gallows and brought back to life to serve Morbidea alone. To them she was a goddess and there was nothing they would not sacrifice for her. As he watched the camp from his vantage place he suddenly felt the point of a sharp dagger poking dangerously at the base of his neck.

'I hope you have good intelligence for us, spy. If not, I might have to let my sisters tear you to pieces.'

'Stinkeye, I might have known you'd be about. Do you never sleep?'

'When you have been dead as long as I have, you do not want to waste time sleeping,' smirked the commander of the Cadaveran nuns. 'Come with me, the queen awaits you and you had better prove yourself worthy. We have been camped here for too long and have other matters to attend to.'

'Tell me, Stinkeye,' asked the spy as they walked to the camp. 'I'm curious to know why you were given that name?'

'I was lucky. I was the first of the sisters to be resurrected by the queen. Her spell was not perfected as it is now. I was brought back from the dead but was left with an eye that seeps with pus, a pus that stinks. I am proud and honoured because I was created to be the commander of her elite forces.'

'Commander Stinkeye, it does have a certain delight to it.'

Stinkeye spun round pinning the spy against a large rock, her face pushed against his. 'I warn you, spy. When the time comes that you have outlived your usefulness, I will be waiting.'

The spy turned his head from the weeping, stinking orb staring fiercely at him. 'Until then,' he choked, 'shall we move along?'

They walked the rest of the way in silence and soon approached a large black marquee. As Stinkeye approached, two guards clenched their right fists and held them across their chests in salute. They wore black leather-studded tunics belted at the waist and thick liquorice-black leather boots. The uniforms gave them the recognition and respect they craved.

Stinkeye entered first. Inside the marquee iron braziers provided heat and light. A black ebony chair engraved with images of strange beasts and symbols sat in the middle of the large tent, surrounded by seven candelabra each holding a dozen candles. Behind the chair, only just distinguishable, a laboratory burbled and gurgled, vapours and fumes emanating from the darkness. A hypnotic ambient sound like the beat of a child's' heart permeated the space. The spy knew this was where Morbidea worked her magic when away from her castle. A movement, a slight sound and Morbidea emerged from the fumes and seated herself in the chair. Stinkeye clenched her fist over her chest and knelt down on one knee.

'Your Majesty, I have brought the spy, as requested.' Morbidea flicked her wrist in a gesture of dismissal and Stinkeye backed out of the marquee.

Morbidea smiled. 'My spy,' she laughed. 'Remove your cloak, poet, let me see you for what you are.'

Paul of the Lapping Loch removed his cloak. 'Why must you gloat at my predicament?'

'If you have a goat, why not gloat,' teased Morbidea. 'Tell me my little goat-poet, what news do you bring me?'

'Please, will you not let me see her first, it has been so long?'

Morbidea erupted like a volcano, the fires flamed up in the braziers and a wind swept through the marquee blinding Paul with dust and ash.

'Do not bargain with me, bard. I will not be toyed with. You will do as I say or your precious love will die.'

'No! I will, I will do as you say. You cannot destroy such goodness.'

Morbidea cackled. Shaking her head, she looked at Paul as if he were the embodiment of stupidity.

'You really are a pathetic wee poet. Do you think I care about this girl or your love for her. Remember poet, I killed my own sister. I would think nothing of squashing you or the girl who has beguiled you. Now! I ask again, what news do you have for me?'

Paul began his painful betrayal. 'The day after tomorrow, at dawn, the wizard plans to pass through the Yett.

'Excellent! I knew he would come. The fool thinks his magic is strong enough to stop me receiving the power of the tail.'

'He does not travel alone. He has two children with him.'

'Children! What children? What do you know of them?'

'Nothing, they are a brother and sister. All I know is he plans a diversion to draw you after him, allowing the children the chance to escape your vigilance.' For a twitch of a second Paul thought he saw a flicker of fear.

'They must be of the blood,' she gasped. 'They have come for the tail. Tell me all, poet, or your precious girl will be given to my Cadaverans.'

'That is all, I swear. There is only the wizard, the two children and their beasts.' Morbidea rose from the chair and paced rapidly back and forth.

'Beasts! What beasts? What creatures do they bring with them? Tell me!' she snapped.

'An owl, a border collie and a horse. A grey mare.'

'This mare, does it have a tail?'

'I don't know, I didn't see it.'

'Guards! Guards!' Morbidea's cry was urgent. The guards rushed in with swords drawn.

'Majesty?'

'Fetch Stinkeye. Get her here now, quickly!' The guards disappeared in haste. 'You have done well, poet. Now, you shall have your reward.' Morbidea raised her arm and pointed at Paul. A bolt of steel blue light shot from the ring on her finger enveloping him in a dark thunderous cloud. The storm haze slowly abated leaving a white luminosity where Paul had stood.

When Stinkeye arrived she gave no thought to the fact that the poet was no longer present.

'You summoned me, Majesty?'

'Is my army ready?'

'Yes, Majesty! The gatherings are complete. We have two more Cadaveran regiments who have sworn to serve you to the second death.'

'Excellent. You have done well, Stinkeye.'

'There is one small thing, Majesty, General MacMorna has made it known he considers my troops an abomination to his professional army. He intends to leave my Cadaverans in reserve when making the final assault.'

'Really? Perhaps I should have him arrested and appoint you supreme commander.' For a moment Stinkeye could not hide her excitement before realising Morbidea had been toying with her.

'The general will obey my orders,' cackled Morbidea. 'Trust me. Your troops will be in the vanguard. What news of the tail?'

'Safe within the walls of our nunnery,' replied Stinkeye, trying to hide her disappointment. 'It is ready for the final ceremony and the imbuing of its power upon yourself majesty.'

'After years of preparation the ceremony will at last take place in the great hall where I dispatched my sister. With the tail as my talisman, I shall lead my armies through the Yett, expanding my realm onto the surface of the Earth, on the night of the Samhain, the night of all dark powers.'

'Yes, your Majesty, and your destiny to destroy the Druid legacy and avenge Morrigan will follow. My sisters and I will ride by your side, for there are many scores to be settled.'

'Indeed there are. First, we must focus on the final preparations and make sure that nothing jeopardises our plans. Listen closely. The day after tomorrow the wizard plans to pass through the Yett. He will attempt to lure you away. I want you to divide your forces, let him think you are following him but leave the fiercest of your Cadaverans close to the portal as others will be following close behind him.'

'Who are they, Majesty?'

'Two children. . . children of the blood.'

Stinkeye's alarm was tangible. Her eye began to seep badly and a note of panic wavered in her voice. 'The prophecy! The children of the blood will come.'

'That concerns me not. If I heeded prophecies, I would not be queen. I return tonight to my castle. You will capture the children and bring them to me.'

'No, Majesty, please! You must let us kill them immediately. As long as they are alive they are a threat to you.'

'I want them alive. On the night of Samhain, at the height of the ceremony, they will meet their end. Their life blood will curdle in the veins of the demon and all who share this blood shall perish with them.'

'Yes. I see, Majesty, by killing all who remain in one fell swoop, the curse will be broken for all eternity.'

'Go now. Be in place before the dawn.'

Stinkeye bowed low backing from the marquee as Morbidea smiled in anticipation of her final preparations.

Chapter 9

PLAN OF ESCAPE

In the entrance hall of a large manor house, the figure of a young man appeared out of a white luminosity – a handsome man with dark wavy hair and blue eyes fit to gaze once more upon the woman he loved. With his heart already pounding, he climbed the wide marble staircase and reached the familiar door to Eilean's chambers. Although this was her prison it was rich and comfortable. Morbidea was treating her well. Paul silently turned the key in the door. Quietly closing it behind him, he stood for a moment looking across at the young woman who had bewitched him since childhood. She was sitting quietly with Heather, their hands and eyes intent on the garments they were sewing.

'Is there no welcome for an old friend?' asked Paul.

'Paul!' Eilean leapt up casting the garment to the floor and rushed to fling her arms around him. Grabbing his hand she dragged him toward the fire. Heather rose from one of the fireside sofas.

'So, Paul,' Heather smiled, 'Morbidea lets you visit us once more. It is good to see you. We always look forward to the news you bring, even though it is seldom encouraging.'

'Good evening, Heather. It is good to see you too.' Paul could not easily disguise the fact that he blamed Heather for what had happened. 'The news I bring is no different from before. Nothing has changed really.'

'How are my father and brother?' asked Eilean. 'Are they well?'

In all of his visits Paul had never revealed the curse that had been cast upon the clan. He didn't want to upset Eilean and was ashamed that the curse had turned him into a traitor and a spy.

'They are well and send you both their love. We are working hard to try and get you back.' They sat and talked for a short while. Paul always found the conversation hard. His dishonesty made him uneasy always trying to remember the lies he had told in case he was caught out. He hated the false situation and what he had become, although he never wanted their meetings to end or to return to the despicable form that awaited him. He shook the thoughts from his mind and picked up the garment Eilean had been sewing.

'What are you working on? From what I remember you never liked sewing before.' The girls drew closer and Eilean whispered conspiratorially.

'We are making breeches for ourselves. Heather and I plan to escape but we'd never get far in these ridiculous dresses.'

'Escape?' gasped Paul. 'No, you will put yourselves in too much danger. We do not even know where this place is, it might not even be within Morbidea's own realm.'

'True,' said Eilean, leaning forward and taking Paul's hand, 'but we'll never find out by sitting and twiddling our thumbs here.'

'Even if you did escape, how would you survive? Who would protect you?'

'You forget, Paul, I was never a girl who liked playing with dolls. I used to fight with my brother and all his friends. I could beat any of them with a sword and could ride better than all of them put together.'

'I remember. It really annoyed them that you could best them every time.'

'Besides,' continued Eilean, 'Heather was taught how to use the faerie bow. She could put an arrow through an apple from two hundred yards. If we escape we will be able to defend ourselves.'

'If you escape we will not be in touch with one another. I will have no idea where you will be.'

'We cannot just sit here and wait, Paul. We have to do something. We know Morbidea is planning a campaign of evil, she is preparing her army.'

'Promise me you will do nothing until after my next visit,' pleaded Paul. 'I might be able to find ways to help you in your escape.'

'I'm sorry Paul. We cannot promise. If the opportunity arises to abscond, we will have to take it.'

'I will try and come again soon. Maybe I can find out information that could help you.'

Paul suddenly became aware of a tingling on the back of his legs, he knew the rough goat hair was growing back.

'I must go now. If I break her rules she will not permit me to visit again. Please be careful. Goodbye.' He embraced Eilean tightly and then shook hands with Heather. 'Please take care of her.'

'I will do my best,' replied Heather.

Paul turned quickly and with a lingering look behind was gone.

Chapter 10

THE DECEPTION

As the children lay asleep on the large bed, the fire burned down in the grate causing the room to become cooler. Fiona woke with a shiver. Crossing to the fire she scratched Kirsty's ears and placed two logs onto the embers. The flames soon caught and began warming the room once more. Finn was still asleep. It had been a long day and Fiona had many thoughts in her head. A muffled knock at the door brought her back to the present. Kirsty was already sniffing at the bottom of the door wagging her tail. Relieved by this Fiona tip-toed over and quietly opened it.

'May I come in?' Leachim asked. He carried a cloth parcel and placed it on the bed. 'These are for you,' he said.

'What is it?' Fiona opened it and pulled out some leggings, a rough feeling tunic, a dark green cloak and a pair of well-cobbled boots.

'You will find they are much more practical for what lies ahead. There will be times when you will have to move fast and you will not want to be hindered by skirts. There is also a tunic and cloak for Finn. Oh and by the way, we leave tonight.'

'Tonight?'

'Yes. I only announced the day after tomorrow because I knew Morbidea's spy would tell her of our plan. Now we have the advantage.'

'You know who the spy is?'

'Of course. I have known for some time. It is Paul, the poet.'

Fiona was shocked, 'Does the laird know?'

'Of course not.'

'Then why don't you tell him?'

'There would be no point. The laird has enough to deal with. Besides it has allowed me to feed Paul information which will confuse our enemy. They will not be expecting us to pass through the Yett tonight, but once we do they will be alerted and we will have to move quickly. Now, wake up Finn, there is something I must explain to you both.'

Fiona gently roused Finn from his sleep. When he was fully awake Leachim cleared his throat and began.

'Tonight, we pass through the Yett and you must be prepared, you must know what to expect. The Yett is no ordinary portal. It will only be open to us for a very short time and we cannot hesitate or our quest will fail before we even begin. Do you both understand what I am saying?' The children nodded apprehensively. 'The Yett is a seamless passageway between two different worlds, two worlds separated in space and time. We will be travelling through time into a different dimension. You must trust me and do exactly as I say, when I say it. Understood?' Again the children nodded. 'Excellent. Now, I have spoken with Meg and Mouldy and they know what is expected of them. There is no need to brief Kirsty as she will follow you without question. If all goes well, once we are on the other side, we will rendezvous with an ally of the laird. She has made arrangements for our onward journey.'

'Excuse me!' asked Finn. 'What do you mean if all goes well? What could go wrong?

'Hopefully nothing, but there is a very slight possibility a solar wind could collide with converging magnetic fields. However that is highly unlikely.'

'I hate it when that happens,' joked Finn.

'Finn, be serious. If that were to happen, Leachim, what would it mean for us?'

'It would mean that the portal could close when we were inside it. It would be a bit like having your finger slammed in a very heavy door.'

'I hate when that happens too.'

'Only we would be the finger. Now the only person who knows we are going tonight is the laird. He, along with Tam and Wattie, will escort us before leaving to take up their positions. We will then travel onto the Yett itself.'

'How long will it take us to get there?' asked Fiona.

'Not long. It is closer than you can imagine.'

'I was thinking,' said Fiona, 'it is awful what Morbidea has done to the laird's people, causing them to fight and argue among themselves and turn on us. It makes me ever more determined to succeed. We have to get the tail back and make sure the Yett is closed forever.'

'She would destroy this world and erase its history surely,' added Leachim. 'It would become merely a colony of her dark and evil domain.'

'I do hope the laird does not hang Callum and the others. That would destroy his clan forever and play right into Morbidea's hands.'

'It would destroy the laird forever. Callum is his only son.' Fiona and Finn gasped.

'He can't do it. He wouldn't hang his own son!' cried Fiona.

'He can't be seen to be weak or show favouritism. If he did, others would challenge his authority and all order would crumble. His people are tired and desperate. Some really believe Morbidea will reverse her spell when she has conquered our world.'

'The laird respects you, Leachim; speak to him and make him postpone any execution at least until we return.'

'I have already done so, Fiona, and I think he will consider it. He knows that no good can come from it but his hands are tied.' Leachim crossed to the door. 'Now I have things to see to and Kirsty must join with Meg and Mouldy. Come girl,' Kirsty obeyed. 'Until tonight my young friends.' The door closed and he was gone.

Finn wandered over to Fiona and nipped her hard on the upper arm.

'Ouch! What was that for?'

'I just wanted to make sure we weren't dreaming,' he laughed.

'You're supposed to nip yourself, you daft gowk.'

'I know that,' he said, 'but it hurts too much.'

'It's a bit scary not knowing what lies ahead,' said Fiona, 'I wonder what will become of us.' Finn had picked up a small curved stick of firewood and put the end in his mouth, just like a pipe.

'Well,' he said, 'if all goes well and the solar wind from the dog's bottom doesn't meet a magnet, then we shouldn't get squashed like a thumb in a door.' Fiona guffawed. Finn's voice and actions were a perfect impersonation of the wizard. Fiona had always been amazed how Finn could mimic people even after only meeting them for a short while. He carried on.

'I think I can persuade the laird not to hang the young goat.'

'Don't, Finn. It's not funny, I shouldn't be laughing but you're so good at copying people.'

'I know. I'm only doing it because it makes me laugh too, even though there doesn't seem to be much to laugh about.' Finn's voice saddened.

'Come here,' Finn went to his sister and they held each other in a close hug. 'Don't worry, we'll be fine. We'll take care of each other.' Fiona's voice was reassuring but her thoughts were less so.

Chapter 11

LEAP OF FAITH

In the dead dark of the night Leachim collected the children from their chamber. He arrived carrying a long canvas sheathe strapped over his back, his staff in his hand and a flaming torch.

'It's time, my young friends, let's go.'

He led them through dim passageways that gently climbed uphill further into the labyrinth of caves. The air was humid. Their progress was swift. No one spoke. As they advanced the air began to cool. Fiona sensed they were nearing the outside. Ahead of them they could see torches that flamed brightly; they danced with the rhythm of a gentle breeze. Shadows moved on the walls of the cave. When they got closer they saw it was the laird waiting with Wattie and Tam.

'Good,' exclaimed the laird. 'So far all is well. The animals are already in place.' Wattie and Tam stood aside revealing a fissure in the rock above where fresh air was breathing into the cave. Looking up the children could see a patch of sky. It was still night and there was a glimpse of glistening stars. 'Now let's take up our positions.'

Leachim unslung the long canvas sheathe and opened the end. From it he pulled three ornate staffs, each with a large clear crystal set on the top. He handed these to the laird and his helpers.

'Good luck,' wished the laird as he shook hands with the three adventurers, then he and his men climbed nimbly up through the fissure and disappeared into the starry night.

Leachim followed. He climbed steadily followed by Finn who watched exactly where to put his hands and feet. Fiona followed Finn, glad of her new clothing. She would have found the climb very cumbersome in a dress.

They emerged into the night and found themselves on the top of a high ridge. The air was clear and crisp and a welcome change to the stuffy humid air of the caves. The blanket of stars above them stretched to the ends of the heavens, the full moon illuminating the tranquil night-time landscape to the far edge of the horizon. Fiona's soul soothed as she inhaled the air. Finn stretched, arousing a renewed sense of energy and purpose.

'You are doing well,' pronounced Leachim striding ahead. The children fell in behind him. Fiona glanced around making a mental note of the precise position of the cave's exit. Marching forward, she became increasingly grateful of the freedom her new clothes gave and vowed never to wear a dress again.

As they rounded the base of a jagged rock face, there in front of them stood Meg, her grey coat shining ghost-like in the moonlight. A silver silhouetted owl perched on her head and her four-legged friend sitting faithfully at her feet. It was a sight that could have seriously spooked any other traveller. Finn ran over and clapped and kissed Meg's nose; Kirsty gave a jealous jump for attention. Meg wore the laird's double saddle strapped to her back, with the two sets of stirrups hanging by her sides.

Leachim wasted no time. 'Finn, climb up into the front saddle. Fiona, you get up behind.'

Earnestly the children obeyed. Leachim took Meg's halter and led them towards the distant sound of flowing water. Kirsty followed. From their vantage point in the saddle Finn and Fiona could see the waters of the river, black, silver and menacing. Leachim halted his crew at the edge of the river, turning to give the children a reassuring nod.

'Is this the Yett?' asked Fiona, raising her voice to be heard.

'No,' Leachim yelled back, 'but the river will carry us to it.'

Finn shifted in his saddle. 'You mean we're going into the river. It looks deep. We could get swept away.'

Leachim laughed. 'That is the plan, Finn. We are going over the top of the waterfall.'

'What? That's stupid,' cried Finn. 'It's hundreds of feet, we'll all be killed before we even get...'

Leachim silenced Finn with a blazing gaze. 'You promised to do exactly as I asked. Now, no more questions, absolute obedience is required.'

Fiona placed her hands on Finn's shoulders and gave him a reassuring squeeze. 'It's all right. We must do exactly as he tells us from now on. Don't be afraid. We are all together.'

Leachim, leading Meg by the halter, stepped from the riverbank into the water. He had done this many times and knew the underwater terrain well. He continued to walk and soon the water level was up to his chest. Even on Meg's back the water reached over Finn and Fiona's knees. Once in the middle of the river, Leachim carefully turned Meg so that they faced downstream to the crest of the waterfall. Fiona noticed Kirsty was having trouble staying with them so she grabbed her by the rough of her neck and pulled her up between herself and Finn. Fiona could feel the water surge past. The blood in her veins was coursing even faster. She had never known such excitement, such exhilaration. Finn shivered with the thrill of danger and delight.

'I'll never complain about having a bath ever again,' he said bravely.

'Dawn is with us,' proclaimed Leachim. 'Be ready, it is time.'

The sun had begun to rise. The horizon before them paled and chased the night sky. On top of a hill to the north of the loch a movement caught Fiona's attention. It was a figure she presumed to be the laird. Turning in her saddle she noted two similar figures, one to the south and the other to the west.

Leachim, continuing to hold Meg's halter, raised his staff high into the air. He was watching for the exact moment the centre of the sun would clear the eastern surface of the Earth, when the flare would be at its strongest.

His eyes waited. His voice called out.

'Widdershins an' widdershins
Aboot this earth we'll go
An' nane will ken whit we hae done
In the shadows doon below
Sae open noo this ancient yett
As the sun flares in the heavens
An' let the bairns o' the blood flood through
Tae fight for the land o' the living.'

Leachim's timing was perfect. The sun cleared the horizon causing its light to flare and focus as if through a lens. The shaft of light shot towards the crystal on Leachim's upheld staff, lighting it up like a thousand chandeliers. It fired three arrows of light towards the crystals being held aloft by the laird and his men. From north, south and west the rays of light deflected and converged on the compass centre above the surface of the loch causing a massive explosion. Water spumed in a surge of energy high into the air. As the eruption subsided a large wave swelled violently over the surface of the water. Fiona and Finn watched in absolute awe as the tsunami swept towards them. The water around them rose.

'Here we go!' they heard Leachim yell as they were sucked like insects down the river and over the crest of the waterfall out into the watery abyss.

Never in the history of the Earth had there been such a scene. Meg, her nostrils flared, struck out with her hooves to no avail, the children on her back. Leachim to her left had let the halter go, arms out, staff in hand, looking as if he had dived from cliffs all his life. To the right, Kirsty had jumped from the saddle in confusion, her tail circling madly as she awaited her fate. Mouldy's feathers were soaked through and all he could do was drop like a wet mop, his wings unable to support him. All except the wizard were filled with the fear that when they hit the surface of the water they would be dead.

Plummeting through the horsetail fan of water, the sun's reflections blinded them with a brightness and clarity that was purifying. The rays shone through the tumbling waters creating the most vibrant rainbows. The intrepid adventurers fell headlong into a spectrum of colour searing past them at the speed of light. Magically and timelessly they fell; travelling in dreamtime through the rainbow's light, their senses informing them a transformation was taking place; their bodies ingesting the colours no longer falling but flying, their physical forms being absorbed by the light.

As the vibrancy of the spectrum dissipated, new surroundings began to materialise before them. For Fiona it was like waking from a wonderful dream, a dream that made you happy. You missed it when it was over but it gave you that glad to be alive feeling. They found themselves in the clearing of a vivid green woodland; the air was sweet with the scent of lilac and jasmine. Unfamiliar luscious plants grew in abundance and the sound of a stream gurgled and tinkled musically nearby. A soft light dappled on the greenery but it was hard to discern where it was coming from. They were all completely dry. Neither their clothing nor any of the animals were wet.

'Wow! What was that?' gasped Finn.

'We are here in the land of our allies,' replied Leachim. 'The only race that will help us in our quest against Morbidea.'

Fiona took a deep breath and looked around the clearing. 'It's so beautiful. Who is it that lives here?'

'There will be time for explanations later. Dismount quickly, danger lurks close by. Mouldy, we need a quick reconnaissance flight of the area, if you please. Make sure my ruse to fool the Cadaverans has worked.' Mouldy took off silently and disappeared into the trees, banking and swooping as he went. 'It will not be long before they know we have passed through the Yett. Let us be gone from here quickly. Follow me.'

Leachim strode forward with his staff held in front of him and as he did so the dense growth of foliage, grass and bushes instantly parted allowing the travellers through, closing immediately behind them, covering their tracks. They were through the Yett and their quest had begun in earnest.

Chapter 12

LAND OF DANGER AND DELIGHT

Stinkeye was in her commander's quarters bathing her suppurating orb when she was given the news. Her eye had been seeping badly and she'd had to dispose of her favourite patch which had become encrusted with puss. She had cut new eye-patches from the fleece of a lamb that she had kept in a pen until it died from thirst. She believed this would make the patches more absorbent. As she tied the patch in place, Seneca, the army's seer, rushed into her tent.

'What do you want Seneca? Haven't you heard of knocking?

'Have you tried knocking on canvas? Nobody ever hears you. Anyway, there is no time for knocking. The Yett has been breached; there have been deflections in the light prism. The wizard has passed through!'

'What? Then the poet has deceived us. He was not meant to pass through for two days yet. We must get after them. Guard!' A Cadaveran guard rushed into the tent and stood to attention. 'Sound the alarm, everyone to horse and send Slimonica to me at once.' The guard quickly saluted and left.

'Shall I send a messenger to inform Morbidea?'

'No! She has already begun her journey back to the castle. Let us deal with this.'

'The queen will blame you for this Stinkeye. You should have left a guard at the clearing.'

'And you, Seneca, you are supposed to warn us of such things. Morbidea will not count you as blameless. It is in both of our interests to sort this out. They will be heading to Antler Pass to make their way through the mountains. We must stop them there.' The tent flap was thrown back and a thin emaciated Cadaveran soldier nimbly stepped in.

'You sent for me, commander?'

'Slimonica! You are the swiftest of my troops; take three of your best sisters and ride fast to Antler Pass. Stop anyone trying to take the path through the mountain into our lands. Watch for two human children, a boy and a girl. Show no mercy. Kill them immediately. When you have succeeded report back to me and not a word of this to anyone.'

'Very good commander,' responded the slender assassin as she slipped from the tent.

Above the camp of the Cadaverans, Mouldy circled inconspicuously watching as the garrison alarm was sounded and the squadron hurriedly saddled their horses. He banked away content that his friend Leachim and the children had a head start over these wretched creatures. What he didn't see was the four swift horses that had left ahead of the rest.

Leachim and the children had been travelling through the forest with ease. The path was wide and the ground underfoot was soft but firm. Leachim seemed in no mood for talking and pressed on with a determination that did not encourage any questioning from the children. Finn was holding Meg's halter and Fiona walked beside him. He tugged her sleeve.

'This place is nicer than I thought it was going to be.'

'This isn't Morbidea's land. This is the land of Leachim's allies. I don't think we'll be staying here too long, Finn.'

'Where do you think this is then?' he asked.

'I think this is the land of the faerie people.'

'The baby stealers?'

'I don't know. I think their main task is the same as the laird and his men. I think they must guard this side of the Yett. That is why he calls them allies.'

'What is an ally anyway?'

'It is someone who is on your side.'

'If they're on our side how come we haven't met them yet? They didn't even send anybody to meet us.'

'I don't know, but we'll find out soon.'

'I'm getting up on Meg. My legs don't want to walk anymore.' Finn put his foot in the stirrup and swung up onto Meg's back. They tramped on in silence, which was broken only when Meg strode softly up beside Fiona.

'A penny for them,' she said gently.

'I've got so many thoughts, Meg. I don't know where to begin. When did you know all of this was going to happen?'

'Not until the night of the storm,' replied Meg, 'I suppose I had a premonition that things were coming to a head. The wizard came to us in the barn and told us what was likely to unfold. Mouldy and I both knew then we would be coming with you. We only had to wait until morning when you and Finn came over to the barn.'

Fiona laughed. 'Farmyard tasks seem far away now and look how quickly things have happened.'

'I think things will be happening quickly for some time to come.'

Their conversation was interrupted by a bark. Fiona noticed they had cleared the forest and were heading uphill towards a ridge a short distance ahead of them. Kirsty, already on the ridge, was silhouetted against the sky. At the top a stunning panorama over a wide and sparkling loch stretched into the horizon. Far off, spread along the distant shore and casting an icy reflection over the surface of the clear water was a delicate white forest. At the centre stood a magnificent white oak tree that towered high above all the others. They stood awestruck at the beauty of the mystical land before them.

'Is that snow over there?' asked Finn.

This had been Fiona's first thought too, before she realised it was something far more breathtaking.

'You could be forgiven for thinking that, Finn,' rasped Leachim's gruff voice. 'It's not snow, it's camouflage.'

'Camouflage? You can see it for miles.'

'We can, yes, but that is because we are their friends and allies. Come this way.' Leachim turned and took a path leading them down from the ridge and along to the shore of the loch. Fiona held back for a moment and gazed beyond the white forest to the mountains far on the horizon. It was a long way off but the two highest peaks reminded her of stag's antlers. She inhaled deeply, sighed at the wonder of it all before quickly setting off to catch up with the others.

Chapter 13

THE ESCAPE ATTEMPT

On the other side of Antler's Pass, far to the north, Eilean and Heather were planning their escape. They had discovered that they were incarcerated in the house of General MacMorna and therefore knew that they were being held in the capital city of Dunraven. They would have a long and arduous journey ahead of them if escape was successful. They would need to be well prepared.

Events, however, seemed to be aiding their plans. The general was seldom at home as the mobilisation of his army occupied him completely and the task of guarding the prisoners had been handed from a body of his soldiers to his household servants.

With the general away the servants had relaxed and become less diligent in regard to their household duties. One servant, Evano, had taken a particular liking to Heather and had brought her gifts of fruit and wine. A month earlier, when most of the household had the day off and others had gone to the local market, Heather persuaded Evano to give her a tour of the house. She carefully took note of all the rooms and corridors and paced out distances which she committed to memory. Returning to her quarters she had drawn a perfectly detailed map as near to scale as she could remember. That night she and Eilean memorised the entire layout.

Heather told her, 'There was one room, down in the basement, which he avoided. When I asked him about it he told me it was just a storeroom. It was where they kept the old junk, he said, no one really went in there. It was too much information. I could tell he was lying. There was also a door to the outside. I could see daylight seeping from under it and felt a draft blowing in. I think that would be our best way out and we could try checking out the mystery room if we plan well.'

The girls decided they would escape the following week on market day when there would only be a couple of servants in the house.

The morning of the escape they awoke early. After Evano and another servant had taken away their breakfast tray they promptly dressed in the leggings they had made themselves. They had hoarded just enough food to keep them going but not so much as to be encumbered.

A short while later, satisfied that the other servants had gone to the market, the girls put their plan into action. Kneeling by the door Eilean could see that the key was in the lock on the other side. Evano had locked the door behind him as always and the key had been left slightly turned. Eilean took a long darning needle and inserted it into the lock. Carefully she manoeuvred it against the tongue of the key and tried to coax it to straighten up. After a series of frustrating attempts it finally moved into the position she required.

Heather passed her a square of linen material which had two long narrow knitting needles sewn into the seams. She slipped this under the door until it was positioned below the key on the other side.

'Wait,' whispered Heather. She lay on her front and put her index fingers under the end of the knitting needles and pressed with her thumbs to raise the linen off the floor slightly. 'Just so it doesn't bounce too much. Right, go for it.'

Eilean carefully pushed the key from the lock listening intently. She heard nothing. Looking at Heather she asked, 'Did you feel it?'

'No. Did you do it?'

'Yes.'

'Have a look.'

As Heather slowly pulled the material back into the room the key appeared lying plump in the middle of the linen square.

'Yes!' cried Eilean as she snapped it up. Heather's plan had worked and the girls screamed silently, ecstatic in their success. Slinging their little sacks of food over their shoulders, they listened carefully before unlocking the door. Opening it quietly, Heather peaked out. There was no one about. They slipped into the hall closing and locking the door behind. Eilean put the key into the pocket of her leggings.

They made for the end of the hall, turned right then descended a stairwell that led to the basement area of the house. It was very dark and no candles or lamps were burning. Heather closed her eyes and conjured up the layout in her head. After a second she took Eilean's hand.

'This way.' She moved off feeling her way along the wall. They passed by some large wine racks which she recalled. 'The door to the outside is at the end of this corridor,' she whispered. 'We should come to a stack of barrels opposite the locked room. We'll take a look in.'

As they approached the door it opened unexpectedly and a light from a lantern spilled into the corridor. The girls instinctively ducked behind the barrels and froze, hardly daring to breathe. They heard someone whistling softly and Evano appeared from the room. A reassuring squeeze of each other's hands confirmed they had not been seen. Evano closed the door and locked it with a large key. The girls peeped carefully from their hiding place. Evano held his lantern high and placed the large key in a recess in the wall. He took a stone from the top of a barrel and placed it into the recess hiding the key. Hanging the lantern from a hook he blew out the flame and, whistling idly, strolled along the corridor, passing the girls in the dark before disappearing up the stairwell. The girls emerged from behind the barrels when the coast was clear.

'That door he came out of, that is the mystery room,' whispered Heather.

'And we know where they hide the key,' sang Eilean in a childish murmur.

'You're quite enjoying this, aren't you?'

'Yes,' beamed Eilean. 'It's exciting. Let's see what's in there.'

'We'll open the outside door first, make sure we can definitely get out,' suggested Heather. 'It should be along here.' As they slipped further along the corridor a slither of light shone across the flagstones from beneath the door. The key was in the lock and turned easily, suggesting it was used regularly. The door opened inwards and led out onto a courtyard at the back of the house. They left the door ajar and returned to where the lantern hung. Below the lantern on top of a barrel lay a taper and flint. They struck the flint, ignited the taper and, retrieving the key, they unlocked the door and slipped into the room. Neatly stacked along the walls were swords, shields, spears and all sorts of weaponry.

'It's the armoury,' whispered Heather in amazement. 'That's a bit of luck. I think we should help ourselves. I don't think the general would want his guests to be unable to defend themselves. Let's see what we might need.'

They began to search for what might be of most benefit to them. In one corner were a pile of leather uniform tunics, the same as those worn by the general's men. They rummaged until they found two which fitted best along with a pair of boots each. Heather chose a finely made bow and a pouch that held about two dozen arrows. Eilean selected a sword belt with a nicely balanced blade then slung a shield across her back. They also grabbed a couple of helmets. Once equipped, they bravely stepped outside the room and Eilean locked the door and popped the key into her pocket.

'Are you starting a collection?' mocked Heather as she placed the stone back in the wall.

'If they discover we have escaped we don't want them getting in there and arming themselves before coming after us.'

They quickly slipped on the tunics and helmets and Eilean buckled her sword belt around her waist before stepping from the door out into the empty courtyard. Across the cobbled yard was an entrance to the stables.

Eilean smiled wickedly, 'Do you think we should chance stealing a couple of horses?'

'It would be foolish not to check it out,' affirmed Heather. 'I think we've been pretty lucky so far.'

They strode across the yard, their new attire encouraging them to walk with an air of confidence and authority. It was quiet. There was no sign of anyone, only three horses munching lazily in their stalls. Unexpectedly a snorting groan came from an empty stall. Eilean's hand went to the hilt of her sword as they moved forward to see what it was. There, on a bale of hay was a huge lump of a man. He lay on his back, a round mound of a belly rising and falling to the rhythm of his deep snoring. The girls stopped. Heather mouthed that they should slip away quietly and was about to back off when Eilean took a run at the man and kicked his boot. Nothing happened.

'Are you crazy?' whispered Heather in a panic. 'What are you doing?'

Eilean whispered quickly to Heather, 'You go and stand in the shadows.' She kicked again, harder this time. 'Wake up, you lazy dog. Get up now,' she barked in a sharp angry voice.

The snoring hulk snorted and wobbled slightly. 'I said get up, you oaf. Wake up now!'

Heather could not believe what Eilean was doing. The lolling lump rolled off the hay bale, groggy and unsure what was happening. Eilean yelled at him again, 'What do you think the general will say when he hears you've been neglecting your duty?' The mention of the general seemed to have an alarming effect on the rotund stable hand as he wobbled again, this time in fear.

'Sorry,' he stammered, 'I didn't know. . . I was. . .'

'Stop stammering and get two horses saddled right now or by Morbidea's blood we'll have you thrown in a dungeon until the general decides what to do with you.' The befuddled man lumbered faster than he had ever lumbered in his life. He saddled the horses quicker than he had ever done before, all the time apologising and pleading with the kind officers not to get him into trouble. In his stupor the soldiers' tunics and the mention of the general had sent him into a blind panic. Once the horses were ready he held out the reigns in his massive podgy hand. Eilean grabbed them slapping his hand away. 'Now get out of my sight. Count yourself lucky I am in a good mood today or I would tell the general.'

The poor brow-beaten figure backed away, bowing up and down as much as his belly would allow. The girls mounted their beasts, trotted out into the courtyard and set off down the road away from the house.

'You are mad,' exclaimed Heather. 'Absolutely stark, raving mad.'

'I'm not mad,' objected Eilean. 'I just don't like the idea of walking.'

The two young women burst into laughter as they galloped off. They were free.

Chapter 14

VOYAGE OF THE WHITE ARROW

Fiona made a point of catching up with Leachim. There had been a number of questions she wanted to ask. As he led them down from the ridge to the shores of the loch she pressed him for answers.

'As you will no doubt have guessed, we are in the land of the faerie people,' Leachim confided. 'Soon we will meet their queen. She has devised a plan to enable you to enter deep into Morbidea's realm. Our party would be conspicuous, so we will split into two groups, each taking a different approach. If possible, we must rescue the tail before Morbidea can receive its power. If not, our quest will be even more challenging than I would have hoped. Look! Our friends come to meet us.'

Fiona looked out over the loch. Speeding toward a jetty further along the shore was a long, sleek white ship. Its oars dipped and pulled as the bow cut through the crystal-clear water.

'Are we going on that boat?' shouted Finn.

'Indeed we are.' Leachim affirmed.

Mouldy had already taken off and circled the ship in a wide loop before landing on the prow. It was obvious from the speed of the craft that it would reach the jetty well before Leachim's band. Indeed the boat had been moored and prepared for its new passengers by the time they did eventually reach the jetty. The prow now faced back out into the loch in preparation for the onward journey. From the stern a wide gang plank for loading provisions reached down to the shore. A small passenger gangplank crossed from the side of the ship to the jetty. 'The White Arrow' was painted in light blue lettering along the side. As they approached Mouldy was sitting on a post beside the jetty, talking to a diminutive character about four feet in height. When the figure saw Leachim he erupted with an energy that belied his size.

'Leachim, you old rascal, long time no see. I dare say you've been up to no good. Are these our guests? You are all welcome. Mouldy here has been telling me all about you. Climb aboard, bairns. I am Oxterguff, piper to the faerie queen. She has sent me to welcome you.'

Finn had been watching the speaker with careful amusement. He was taller than the other crew members but shorter than Finn himself. He wore leather boots the colour of coal, brown trousers and belted round his moss green tunic was a sword and a dagger. His hair and beard were wild and unkempt framing a face with vibrant green eyes that sparkled with energy. Finn took an instant liking to him. He may have been small in stature but in every other aspect he seemed larger than life. He sprang from the gangplank and jogged down to meet them. Kirsty ran towards him, swishing her tail.

'Sit!' he told her and as she sat he gave her a huge bear-like hug around the neck. 'You are a good girl, eh! You and I are going to have an exciting time.' He took both Fiona's hands and held them tight as he scrutinised her face, 'The loyal and feisty Fiona. Welcome, lass. The queen is looking forward to meeting you.'

'To meeting me!' exclaimed Fiona, 'I've never met a queen before, this is very exciting.'

Oxterguff turned to Meg, putting his hand up to hold her bridal. 'Meg! I can only imagine what you have had to endure over the years. Together we will endeavour to right the wrongs visited on you.' He looked up to Finn. 'And you, young Finn. Are you going to sit on that horse all day? Get down here you lazy tyke and shake my hand.' Finn jumped from the horse and took the offered hand. Oxterguff clamped Finn's hand tight and smiled into his eyes. 'Remember, Finn. We all have more in us than we give ourselves credit for.' He shook hands with Leachim who towered over him.

'You've grown,' laughed Leachim.

'And you've grown. . . less ugly,' joked Oxterguff.

Fiona was impressed at how Oxterguff touched the heart and concerns of everyone. Within minutes of meeting he had boosted the spirits of the group and fostered a sense of excitement for the next stage of their journey. He raced to the top of the gangplank then turned to address the assembly.

'Right, everyone aboard. We have a quest to undertake, one that could kill us all.' A huge grin broke over his face and he spread his arms to encompass all present. 'I for one though, can't think of better company in which to die.' Laughing heartily he leapt into the boat.

Once aboard it wasn't long before they were slipping rhythmically through the water, leaving the shore far behind. The crew sang as they rowed, the rhythm of the oars matching that of the song. It told of epic journeys, battles and heroic deeds and it became apparent that this very boat was one of many in the queen's fleet engaged in the fight against Morbidea's evil regime.

Leachim and Oxterguff stood at the prow below an elegant white swan figurehead. They were deep in conversation. Fiona wandered back to her brother who was sitting with the animals at the stern.

'What are they talking about?' asked Finn.

'I don't know, but I get the feeling they want to be left alone,' Fiona replied. 'I suspect they are planning what we should do next.'

'Well, I hope it involves food,' said Finn, his tummy rumbling. 'I'm starving.'

'You're always starving,' said Meg. I wouldn't worry, I'm sure a decent meal will be provided.' Meg didn't sound too excited at the prospect and Fiona picked up on her mood.

'Why do you say it like that, Meg.'

'Because I would bet a bag of oats we have a very long journey ahead of us, far beyond those mountains.' They all looked towards the horizon.

'They're miles away,' gasped Finn.

'That's only the border of the faerie queen's domain,' squawked Mouldy. 'We have to cross those mountains and then travel north through Morbidea's lands. Time is short and we will have to journey fast and undetected if we can. We have a difficult job on our hands, claws and hooves.' Kirsty gave a bark. 'Sorry! And paws,' he added. They looked again to the distant horizon and fell silent.

Once out on the loch the wind picked up and Oxterguff ordered the sail to be hoisted. The oars were shipped, the men stopped singing and lay back taking their rest as the boat sped across the surface of the water. The canvas sail whipped and cracked and the taut ropes hummed as the wind swept over them.

'She has a strong spirit,' confided Oxterguff watching the bow cut through the foam. 'The boy, however, is young. It may have been more prudent to leave him behind.'

'It had to be,' replied Leachim. 'They are both of the blood and their sibling bond strengthens their resolve. He helps keep his sister focused; together they have faith.'

'If they survive,' mused Oxterguff, 'they will be a great asset to their world, as you are my friend.'

Leachim chuckled. 'There are few who would agree with you on that point.'

Oxterguff slapped Leachim on the back. 'I don't need any to agree with me. It's a fact. I see what you have done for both our worlds. And now we have the chance to fight together eh! We shall have exciting times before we die.' He turned to the others at the back and waved furiously as he shouted at the top of his voice, 'We shall have exciting times before we die.' The others could not hear what he said, the wind swallowing his words. They just smiled and waved back with enthusiasm. Leachim laughed heartily. Oxterguff was fearless and if the worst came to pass it would be an honour dying in his company.

Some hours later the shore became more distinct. The sail was lowered and the rowers, with home in sight, increased their efforts. The children could make out a jetty and somewhere among the soft white trees a horn sounded their approach. Fiona imagined that up to six boats could be moored there at any one time although The White Arrow was the only vessel present.

Approaching the jetty Oxterguff gave the order to ship oars. The rudder was pushed hard to starboard and the boat turned one hundred and eighty degrees, killing its speed, leaving it gently reversing into the side of the jetty. Two of the rowers leapt ashore with ropes as they skilfully brought the boat to berth, facing back out into the loch in anticipation of its next voyage.

Once ashore Oxterguff wasted no time in leading the adventurers onto meet the faerie queen. They took a well-travelled path leading from the loch side through the white woods. The canopy of the forest was formed by snow-white leaves, their colour gently descending into tints of the palest mint. Emerald foliage radiated from the shrub layer deepening into mossy luscious greens in the undergrowth. The shades and hues of the plants and petals were magnificent and the scents and smells were unlike anything Fiona had ever inhaled. Kirsty's nose was working hard registering the aromas. There was so much to see that was new it was hard to know where to look next.

Finn turned in the saddle and leaned down to speak to Fiona. 'This place is magical. It's not like a real forest is it?'

'I know what you mean, it's as if it's listening to us.'

'I'm not scared, it feels good.' Finn turned back in the saddle and as he did so his foot slipped from the stirrup. He fell headlong from Meg's back and was heading for a large rock when suddenly, arm length ferny fronds flipped out beneath him, catching him gently. They held him suspended above the rock before setting him down safely. Then they began to brush him down and pat him reassuringly, just as his mother might have done after he had fallen. From above, the trumpet head of a golden yellow flower swooped down at Finn and sniffed. It recoiled slightly before it returned, sniffed again and squirted him with a sweet-scented spray. The frond arms dusted him down once more then lifted him back onto Meg's back. Finn for once was speechless. As he sat with his mouth open, he was sure the fern was waving goodbye.

'Did that just happen?' asked Finn, his face a little pale.

'That plant saved you from a nasty crack on the head.'

'I know. This might sound crazy, but I think it liked me.'

'I think it thought you were a stinky wee urchin.

'It's made me smell like a lady's hanky now.'

'Maybe it's just as well, you are going to meet a queen remember.'

'Not far now,' shouted Oxterguff as he led them on at a stout pace.

The group travelled on for some time through the thick forest. The terrain gradually opened out onto a wide marshland. It was a natural defensive landscape.

'This is the forward defences of the queen's headquarters,' Oxterguff informed them. One small, narrow path led through the expanse of the marshes to a bridge over a stream. The bridge was guarded by a company of soldiers camped on the other side.

A lookout who spotted the advance of the menagerie sounded a horn. The camp erupted into activity. Within seconds, a phalanx of archers had formed up, crossed the bridge and deployed to face the oncoming travellers. As Oxterguff neared the bridge he stepped forward and raised both arms in the air.

'It is I, Oxterguff, piper to the faerie queen. These are my guests and the queen is expecting them.'

The commander of the archers strode forward. 'Guffy, we thought it might be you, but it never does any harm to practise turning out the guard.'

'Bendbow, it is good to see you are always at the ready.'

Bendbow was another of Oxterguff's clan, with huge arm muscles, not from rowing but from years as an archer.

'Much has happened since you left,' Bendbow informed him as they made their way over the bridge. 'I know not what. There are many rumours but I do know that preparations for war have been speedily put in place. I for one cannot wait to deal with Morbidea and her forces. Is it true you are to go on some secret mission?'

'No! That is a rumour I would be grateful you would squash if you hear it repeated.'

'Consider it squashed. So you are going on a mission? May the strength of the clan bring you success.'

'Success or not it will not be long before we stand beside each other in battle I think.'

'I long for that moment. Now speed you to the queen.'

Chapter 15

QUEEN OF THE FAERIES

By early evening Leachim and his followers had arrived at the domain of the faerie queen. An archway of woven branches and intertwined vines created an intricate and majestic entrance.

'There is no doubt this is the land of the faeries,' Fiona whispered to Finn. 'Everything is so beautiful. It feels familiar, like the stories in the chapbooks Mum got for us.'

'Maybe the person who wrote the stories has been here,' put in Finn, 'I hate to think the next place we visit could be full of old, dead, stinky nuns.'

Oxterguff led them up a wide, crumbling, stone staircase that opened onto a large circular amphitheatre. The performance space was open to the elements and carved pillars and mythical statues stood around the circumference.

It must be thousands of years old thought Fiona. At least ten thousand, no one really knows. Leachim's voice sounded in her head and Fiona smiled over at him.

An ancient moss-covered well sat embedded in the centre of the arena. Four entrances were set like equidistant points on a compass. Oxterguff and his followers arrived from the south and, as they did, so three Celtic lasses appeared, one at each of the other entrances. They were dressed in long silk dresses; one blue, one green and the third red. Their presence created an air of elegance, beauty and calm; their dresses added a solidity to their translucence. Long hair woven into intricate plaits hung to their waists. They were quite the most splendid creatures Fiona had ever seen. Moving gracefully they crossed in unison towards the well.

Oxterguff bowed low. 'Good day, my ladies, may I introduce you to our guests?'

He did so leaving Leachim out of the formalities which Fiona took to mean that they were already known to one another.

'Greetings children,' harmonised three female voices.

'I am Alba,' said the lass in blue. 'These are my sisters, Éirean and Cymru. We are the princesses of the faerie realms that border the dimensions of your world. Our queen bids you welcome and will join you shortly.'

'First you must eat,' instructed Cymru, her red silk dress shimmering in the breeze.

'And drink, to refresh yourselves from your journey,' agreed Eirean.

The three sisters took a step forward and Alba gracefully swept her hand over the top of the well. A soft light emanated from within; a rush of tiny bright faerie creatures flew forth like shooting stars. They were almost transparent and no bigger than the palm of a hand. They glided without wings, moving swiftly from one place to another with lightning ease.

They seemed excited with their task of feeding the guests and laughed and giggled as they did so. The faerie creatures flew swiftly, carrying goblets of golden liquid, plates of sweets and cake which they placed nimbly before the guests. Five of the little creatures hovered before Meg holding a silver bucket bound with gold bands. Meg munched at the delightful faerie delicacies inside. Another flock of faeries flew excitedly around Kirsty dropping treats for her to catch in mid-air, emitting golden giggles as she played their game. Mouldy, Leachim and the children sat on the stone seats encircling the theatre eating and watching with amusement.

'This is the yummiest food I have ever tasted,' said Finn devouring each mouthful.

'There's nothing like this where we come from,' agreed Fiona as she swallowed the glorious honey-tasting mead from her goblet.

When they had eaten their fill the plates and goblets were swiftly collected and the faeries disappeared as quickly as they had arrived.

'Now it is time for you to meet our queen,' announced Alba. 'Sisters, are we ready?' The three lasses took their places around the well. Immediately the mossy stones began to shift forming small steps which the princesses ascended. Taking a step from the top of the wall the girls held hands, forming a circle above the centre of the well. Revolving slowly at first the red, green and blue of their gowns flowed together. As they spun faster and faster they suffused forming a brilliant white light. From this blinding radiance appeared the form of a striking woman.

The queen of the faeries stood majestically before them. The bodice of her dress was a lattice of green and gold, the skirt a simple deep green velvet with a hint of gold embroidery decorating the hem. Long trailing sleeves were cut to midway on her forearms revealing the most exquisite wrists and hands. Locks of wavy hair framed a face that was both beautiful and strong, yet there was sadness in her eyes suggesting a queen who had performed deeds that had torn her soul. As she spoke her voice sang with warmth and wisdom.

'Leachim, it is always good to welcome you, a true friend to my people.'

She stepped forward to greet him. Leachim nodded, gave a low bow and reached out to kiss the queen's hand – a hand that had over time plucked bow, harp and heart strings. He struggled to release his touch on her and Fiona felt that this was the woman for whom Leachim had given up his earthly world. A woman he would never be able to win.

'I am honoured as always to serve you.'

'And these are your friends, Finn and Fiona? We are most happy to have you here with us. I admire the courage you have shown.'

Fiona gave a small curtsey and Finn, who was still dumbstruck by the three princesses and the faeries, copied Fiona and gave a quick bouncing bob of a courtesy. Finn looked so awkward that Fiona couldn't help laughing out loud. The queen smiled.

'Pleased to meet you,' Finn blushed.

'As I am you,' replied the queen. 'You are all welcome. We should talk together as there is much to discuss; come join me at the well. This is the Well of the Abyss, it reaches deep to the centre of our world. Its source inspires us with the wisdom and knowledge of our ancestors; from the abyss we will draw the strength and fortitude needed to help you on your journey. Much has changed since you travelled through the Yett. Much since Oxterguff set off to bring you here and because of this we must change our plans accordingly.'

'We should set off for the mountains right away,' interjected Oxterguff, 'get through Antler Pass as quickly as we can and waste no more time.'

'It is too late for that Oxterguff. Morbidea's people know that the children of the blood have breached the Yett.'

'How can this be?' snapped Oxterguff. 'Have we no element of surprise? How do they know this?'

'Calm yourself Oxterguff. They have a spy in the camp of our allies. One who has told them of our plan; however we can turn this to our advantage.'

Fiona was impressed by the queen's calm nature. With time being so short she had not wasted any of it in anger or regret. She already had another plan.

'Stinkeye, the Cadaveran commander has sent a unit of her swiftest nuns to seal off Antler Pass. They expect this to be the route you take. So we will divide our group. Oxterguff will travel by boat with Fiona, Finn and Kirsty across Quill Cavern, the underground lake. You will rendezvous with the others on the far side of the mountains and journey together from there.'

'Excuse me.' Finn hadn't liked the sound of Quill Cavern. He didn't think it sounded like a very nice place and felt some kind of clarification might put his mind at rest. 'Why is it called Quill Cavern? '

'Because it is as black as an inkwell down there,' Oxterguff informed him. 'It gets dark and deep very quickly. Who knows what creatures inhabit it. If you fall in and are not rescued at once you are done for.'

'Thanks, just what I wanted to hear.'

'It will be safer than you think, Finn,' assured the queen.

'Morbidea's people do not know the lake exists. It is the others who will have a more hazardous journey.'

'If you don't mind me saying so, I was going to mention,' said Meg, 'that a grey horse like myself with no tail might arouse some suspicion.'

'Do not worry, we will use the power of the well to disguise and change your appearances. Leachim, you must travel as your Malcolm self,' instructed the queen. 'Your cover will be that you are travelling to join General MacMorna to fight by his side. You are bringing him a prize hawk as a gift as you know how much he likes hawking. Mouldy will become our hawk.'

'Not much change there,' said Meg. 'One flea-ridden rodent-eater for another.'

'I would like to point out that owls are far more intelligent than any hawk. I take it my intellect will be intact when restored to my natural state of superiority.'

'Indeed it will,' smiled the queen.

'In that case we should turn our attention to the rather large horse in the ointment,' quipped Mouldy, making no attempt to keep the smugness out of his voice.

'Have you all drunk of the faerie mead?' asked the queen.

'They have,' confirmed Oxterguff.

'Then look close and you will see clearly.'

Peering into the surging waters of the cavernous well a theatre of visions swam before them. Epic battles on land and sea swirled to the surface; crashing stories of faerie history rose in the eddies; desperate hands stretched towards them in mournful pleading only to recede back into the deep. A black wind churned the waters to a swell. The sound of beating wings, the cry of predators and the shriek of prey echoed from the depths, followed by a flutter of butterflies, black as night, surging upwards, swarming across the amphitheatre. Black, shining and silky they landed, painting over the visions and settling the waters, returning the turmoil to peace.

The queen stood, her elegant arm pointing towards the southern entrance. There sat Malcolm upon a magnificent, gleaming black mare. Twitching its ear, a solitary black butterfly flapped gently from the horse, fluttered past the children and disappeared down into the well.

Malcolm held the reigns of the horse in his right hand and perched on his gloved left forearm, was a splendid hawk. With a squeeze of his legs the horse moved forward.

'It is good to see you both again,' smiled Malcolm with a glint in his eye.

'And you, sir,' answered Fiona.

'Where's Meg!' shouted Finn, somewhat alarmed.

'Where do you think she is, you daft gowk,' laughed Fiona.

Finn walked forward, 'Meg? Is that you?'

'Aye, it is,' the familiar voice answered. 'I've even got a tail. I'd almost forgotten what that was like,' she announced with a proud swish of her black tail.

'You look amazing. Morbidea's soldiers will never recognise you.'

'Let us hope not,' said Meg.

'Mouldy, you look quite fierce. What's it like being a hawk?' enquired Finn.

'If you don't mind, Finn, I'd rather not open my beak. Being a hawk I might say something stupid and there is a certain hoofed beastie here, who might want to remind me of it in the near future.'

Fiona looked Malcolm up and down. 'You look quite fierce yourself, sir.'

Malcolm was dressed in the black uniform of an officer of MacMorna's army.

'He must look the part,' said the queen. 'I have given him the rank of commander. This way he will outrank most of Stinkeye's Cadaverans, although he will still have to be careful as they do not like taking orders from the general's men.'

'Do we really have to split up?' Finn asked.

'I'm afraid so, but only until we can get you all to the other side of the mountains. Once there you must journey onto Raven's Neuk.

There, you must try and recover the tail before Morbidea can use its power. Now you must rest, for you will leave at daybreak. Good night, my friends, and sleep well, I shall see you on your way tomorrow.'

Oxterguff led the entourage to a large cave the inside of which was strewn with soft grass and foliage. There everyone found a comfortable spot and settled down for the night. One by one they fell asleep. It had been another long and exhausting day. Soon the cave was filled with gentle breathing and twitching paws as a deep sleep engulfed them all.

As the first light seeped into the dying darkness a new dawn was born. Oxterguff arose early and prepared for the day. Then he gently roused the sleeping band. A fire was already burning outside of the cave and an array of breakfast bread and fruit were laid out on a mat. The children knelt and ate in silence listening to Malcolm and Oxterguff as they quietly talked over the plans.

As the day woke up the land, the two bairns were captivated by the delicate beauty of the queen's realm. The green seemed greener than anything on their Earth; the reflections of the early morning light gave a luminous magic extending as far as could be seen.

Meg emerged from the cave, looking magnificent in her new silky black guise.

'Wow! Meg, I forgot you'd been magicked into a different horse. Maybe we should forget the tail and just keep you like this,' joked Finn.

'Suits me fine,' replied Meg, 'I feel as though I could gallop like the wind all day.'

'Unfortunately we need your old tail back,' added Fiona. 'Besides, you might get too big-headed if you stay like that.'

'Her head is big enough as it is,' squawked Mouldy as he landed between Meg's ears. 'I'll never be short of a landing ground as long as she's around.'

Meg looked up at the newly transformed hawk. 'I see you haven't lost what you call your sense of humour.'

'No I haven't lost it, but I'm not as quick-witted as I was yesterday. Hawks really are quite stupid. I look forward to becoming my wise clever self again.'

'I can't wait for that either. Your hawk claws are much sharper than your owl ones.'

'Well, I can't wait for you to become an old nag again. At least then you had a few fleas that I could nibble on.'

Meg shook her head so quickly that Mouldy was completely dislodged and had to flap unceremoniously to the ground.

Chapter 16

THE BOW AND THE ARROW

Far to the north, Eilean and Heather had made good their escape. The horses they had borrowed were excellent beasts and progress had been swift. Unknown to the girls, the uniforms they had picked bore the insignia of a two-headed falcon, giving them the rank of squadron commanders in the general's elite guard. This would be likely to deter even senior officers questioning them too closely.

The girls decided their cover story would be that they were travelling south to take command of a new unit of archers and train them for the forthcoming conflict.

'We should be able to make our way to Antler Pass and hopefully find a way through it,' explained Eilean. 'Also, if any ask for a demonstration, I daresay none will be able to beat you with a bow. Once we are back in the realm of your people, Heather, I'm sure the queen will help reunite us with my father and the rest of my clan.'

'We have been lucky so far,' agreed Heather. 'Every unit of the general's army is mobilising for battle. Something has happened to make them confident of victory. We must warn the queen and, if we can, try to discover something of their plans.'

'Halt! Keep hands on the reins where we can see them.' The commanding voice was that of a soldier who had appeared on a rock above them. Other soldiers materialised from the cover of surrounding trees and the girls were aware of several soldiers appearing behind them, cutting off any retreat.

'This is a restricted area,' said the soldier in command.

'We are on our way. . .'

'Be quiet! I am not interested in what you have to say. You will come with us. Our colonel will want to question you. Take their weapons,' he barked to his men.

The girls were quickly and deftly unarmed and their horses grasped by their bridles. 'Take them back to camp.'

As they were led off Eilean whispered from the side of her mouth, 'Whatever we do we must stick to our story.'

A few minutes later they arrived at an army encampment in the centre of which was spread a large marquee. As they dismounted it was Heather's turn to whisper.

'There must be at least a thousand troops here, I hadn't expected to see that many this far south.'

Flanked by three soldiers, they were marched into the marquee by the young officer in command. He snapped to attention waiting for his colonel to speak. The colonel, a man with a large imposing frame, turned from a table where he had been studying some charts. Eilean and Heather snapped to attention at exactly the same time. It was an unintended reaction but looked very slick and professional.

'Yes.' The battle-scarred colonel had a hint of annoyance in his voice.

'Colonel Vagrin, we came across these two travelling through the restricted zone. We thought you might wish to interrogate them.' There was an element of toadying in the young officer's voice and Eilean thought she registered a wince of annoyance in the colonel's face.

'What were they doing there?' the colonel snapped.

'I don't know, sir, we brought them straight to you.'

'You mean you didn't ask them?' Vagrin was looking his subordinate straight in the eye, a look which unnerved the young officer.

'I, I thought. . .'

'No, you didn't,' snapped Vagrin. 'If you'd thought you would have questioned them first before bringing them here. If they have a valid reason then you have wasted my time.'

'I. . . I'm sorry. . . I. . .'

'Dismissed, get back to your duties. I'll deal with them.'

The young officer saluted and left the tent followed by his men. Vagrin looked sternly at the two women.

'Stand at ease.'

The two girls did so in absolute unison.

'What are you doing here?'

He listened intently as Eilean gave the colonel the story they had worked out.

'I see you wear the insignia of the two-headed falcon. You are members of the general's elite guard? If the general wants women officers in his elite guard then that is his decision. My own opinion is that the army is no place for women. Times change, eh! Or so I am told.'

An idea flashed in Eilean's mind. She knew that most of the older commanders in the army were fiercely proud of their men and their reputations but there was one development they despised more than anything: Morbidea's Cadaverans were hated and were looked upon as an affront to the real army. Eilean thought she might be able to use this to her advantage.

'We are part of a new unit, colonel. The general does not trust the Cadaverans. He thinks that they will attempt to take control of the army. He has ordered us to watch them closely and be prepared to move against them if they prove disloyal. That is why he has enrolled us into the elite guard.'

The colonel's face reddened and his eyes blazed. It worked, thought Eilean.

'They are an abomination, a disgrace. Does the queen not believe that her own army can protect her, that we cannot carry out her orders? These she-devils care only for revenge against the Earth dwellers. They should be dispatched back to the graves from whence they came.'

'I agree, sir. The unit of archers we have been sent to train will be kept in readiness and stationed close to their quarters. We will be poised and ready to destroy them at the general's command.'

'That is a wise move on MacMorna's part. These archers of yours, how many do they number?'

Eilean was not sure how many archers would be in a normal unit and for the first time in her fabrication she was caught off balance.

'Three hundred,' Heather replied. She knew, being an archer herself. 'They are already well trained but they must be taught to aim for the neck and the heart, those are the areas that will kill a Cadaveran instantly.'

'I have a bad feeling regarding this coming conflict. We have no need to wage war against the Earth dwellers. There is enough to deal with in our own world. There are other arenas in which the army is required. You are the ones that will train these archers?'

'Yes, sir,' answered Heather.

'Then you will show me your technique. I will have you draw against my own best archer and see if you can not only beat him but help him to improve his skills,' the colonel's voice boomed. 'Sleekman!'

Sleekman, the young officer who had arrested them, re-entered the tent and stood to attention. His instant arrival suggested to Eilean that he had been listening to their entire conversation.

'Fetch Shaftsbury to the target range. We are going to have a little competition. Our finest archer against this female officer of the elite guard.'

'Right away, colonel, and I'll wager our man will win.' He hurried from the tent and was heard shouting many orders to carry out the colonel's one.

'It is my greatest hope,' sighed the colonel, 'that he will be killed in his first engagement with the enemy.' The two girls looked slightly shocked. 'I am sorry,' the colonel sighed again, 'but I despair of him, he is all bluster, his men do not like him and I know in the heat of battle he will prove to be a coward.'

Two other guards entered and the girls were led away to the target range. Heather was handed her bow on the way there, although she was given no arrows. By the time they arrived at the target range it was obvious that word had spread. There were over a hundred soldiers all eager for some sport to break the boredom of being in camp. Many were placing bets on the outcome. The target range was five hundred yards long with the forest at the far end. Every one hundred yards there was a marker. The soldiers lined up on either side and the firing position was marked with two red flags. A rope ran along the ground between the flags but there was no sign of any targets.

Shaftsbury was already there. He was of slim build, above average height and had the well-developed arm muscles required to fire a strong bow. Heather noted his keen intelligent eyes and suspected he would be a formidable opponent. As they approached a few voices rose in comment from the watching troops.

'Show these women how to shoot, Shaftie.'

'Tell them it's not knitting needles they're firing.' Laughter followed this last remark. Shaftsbury smiled as the girls stopped before him.

'Pay no attention to them,' he said. 'It's just a bit of fun.'

'I hope you feel that way when Heather beats you in front of all of your friends,' Eilean's comment was designed to test his reaction. 'We wouldn't want you to be too embarrassed.' He looked straight into her eyes and held her gaze.

'I never get embarrassed,' he smiled, 'besides I know I can shoot when I have to. I have nothing to prove, as I am sure your friend hasn't either.' His smile increased and his eyes held hers. Eilean looked away to Heather and was instantly annoyed with herself for not holding eye contact with him; she felt as if she had allowed him to win. But win what she wasn't quite sure.

'Are you ready, Heather?' she asked tersely.

'I am pleased to meet you, Heather, I am Cranan Shaftsbury. Your friend does not believe in introductions. Never mind, we also have rude elements in our squadrons. They can't help it, it's the way they were brought up.' Heather let out a laugh. She could see Eilean was livid and realised she had never seen her bested in an exchange of words before.

Sleekman arrived and handed Heather a quiver of arrows.

'Six arrows each, one each at two hundred yards, one each at three hundred yards and your final four will be on moving targets. It was then the girls noticed two prisoners being led out onto the firing range. Each of them had a round target marked with circles strapped to his back. They were marched to the two-hundred-yard point and made to stand with their backs to the archers.

'What is this?' Eilean asked. 'Who are these men?'

'These men are deserters who have been sentenced to death,' Sleekman put in smugly. 'After the first arrow they will move to the three-hundred-yard spot. After the second arrow they will run the remaining two hundred yards for the woods, they will be your moving targets. If they make it to the woods then they can have their freedom.'

'We didn't agree to this, to shoot your deserters for you.'

'Of course you didn't agree to it. You were ordered to.'

Eilean wanted to slap the smirk off his insolent face but turned her anger to Shaftsbury. 'And you are happy with this?'

'What has happiness to do with it? Those men are to be hanged at dawn. They volunteered for this, at least this way they have a chance.' This time Eilean did not release him from her gaze. She was angry, her fierce eyes burning.

Sleekman's voice broke in, 'May the best... soldier win.'

He tossed a coin and Heather called correctly, letting Shaftsbury shoot first. His bow was larger than Heather's. He loaded his arrow with ease, pulled back seemingly without effort and lifted the bow into place. A second's pause and he released the arrow. The shaft flew straight and true without wavering in a beautiful arched line, the sound of it piercing the air like rushing wind that subsided with a thump as the arrow buried itself into the round black centre of the target. A huge cheer came from the watching soldiers with shouts of praise for their champion. The prisoner who had not moved an inch shuddered visibly.

Heather had let him go first because she wanted to assess his ability. He's good, she thought to herself. Eilean was equally impressed with the shot.

'Now the elite guard will shoot.'

Sleekman could not help but sound a note of derision in his pronunciation of the word 'elite'. Heather took an arrow from her quiver and instantly realised it had been tampered with. Someone had crumpled or crushed the flight feathers. Not a lot, but enough to affect the arrow's flightpath. She held up the quiver as though she was choosing the arrow she would require and blew very gently upon the feathers. A silvery mist from her breath filtered through the feathers and they were combed as by magic into perfect alignment. Taking up her stance she noticed the prisoner was trembling slightly and guessed that Sleekman had given her the more nervous of the condemned men to wear her target. Holding her bow at arm's length across her abdomen she positioned the arrow. Closing her eyes she took a few breaths to become one with her bow and, raising it slowly, she pulled back on the twine until the bow was fully taut and the arrow aligned with her closed eyes. Her breath was calm and slow.

A voice from the crowd cried, 'Get on with it.' He held the silver coin Sleekman had given him but was immediately silenced by a look from Shaftsbury.

Heather had been oblivious to the cry, to everything. Her eyes flicked open and in that instant she released the arrow. It seemed to fly with the speed of a flash of lightning and struck the centre of the target with such force it threw the prisoner forward onto his front. A gasp from the crowd was followed by a second of silence, a cheer and some wild clapping. The soldiers knew a competition was on and some began changing their bets.

The first shots were officially declared a draw. The arrows were removed from the targets and the prisoners moved to the three hundred yards point. Sleekman was annoyed that his cheating had not produced a better outcome.

Shaftsbury took his second shot from the longer distance with the same perfect discipline and scored dead centre once more. Heather stuck to her slow and considered preparation and let fly with an equally centred shot.

It was at this precise point everything changed. Shaftsbury's prisoner sensing the lull before the final shots decided to make a run for the woods. He threw off his target and ran as fast as he could, dodging and turning in different directions to make it difficult to hit him.

Sleekman, sensing that Shaftsbury might have an advantage called, 'The targets are moving, fire your final arrows.'

Heather's prisoner took off like a frightened rabbit. He ran in a straight line towards a gap in the trees, his target still strapped on his back, gambling that it would give him some protection. Shaftsbury knew that, despite the energetic actions of his mobile target, there was only one gap in the woods that he could get through. He would save his shot until then. Heather, on the other hand, didn't want to bring her prisoner down. Shaftsbury's man who had a head start made it to the woods first. As he got to the opening, Shaftsbury let his arrow fly. The man reached the trees and turned in the certainty that no one could shoot accurately at that distance when the arrow struck the tree beside his head. He gave a shriek, gathered his senses and made a rude gesture before disappearing into the woods. Shaftsbury chuckled to himself and the crowd laughed and cheered.

Heather's prisoner was approaching the gap in the woods, running wildly without looking back. Heather's eyes flicked open and the arrow flew straight and true hitting the target once more, sending the prisoner flying forward. He got up, threw the target on the ground, gave the same rude gesture and disappeared into the trees.

'After them,' screamed Sleekman.

'Leave them. They are cowards and I will not have them in my regiment.' The colonel put his arm around Shaftsbury's shoulder and led him over to Heather. 'Your man got away, Shaftsbury.'

'He was just too slippery for me sir.'

'He certainly took us all by surprise,' laughed the colonel. 'She shoots well, don't you think?'

'Indeed, and she would have won. She would have killed her man had he not kept the target on his back.'

'I can see why the general has enlisted you in his elite guard.'

'Colonel, colonel!' a soldier hurriedly approached. 'Look at this.' The soldier held up Heather's target. The arrow she had fired at five hundred yards had hit the centre spot splitting her previous arrow clean in two. The colonel and Shaftsbury looked at it in amazement.

Shaftsbury gave an appreciative whistle. 'That is a first for me,' he exclaimed.

'In my whole career I have never seen the like. Heather, you must teach Shaftsbury that trick,' said the colonel.

'A fluke, I assure you colonel,' smiled Heather, 'A lucky shot, that's all.'

'Sleekman, these soldiers will continue on their way immediately. Get their horses ready and return their weapons to them. See that they get enough provisions to set them up for their journey.'

'Yes, Colonel.'

Sleekman snapped to attention but was seething that he had been ordered to serve two women officers.

Chapter 17

ANTLER PASS

It was in the mid-mirk of early morning when Slimonica and her three comrades slipped into Antler Pass. They manoeuvred their horses along the narrow track, rocks towering above them on either side. The sun rose warming the tops of the mountains; it would be a few hours before its heat would seep into the shadowy pass itself. Heat, however, was not something these previously dead women warriors craved or required. Although they lit campfires in the evenings, they did so only to illuminate their encampments and to provide visibility in the event of a night-time attack.

At noon when the sun was high, the comrades set up camp in a narrow gorge off the main track. They tethered their horses and scouted to find the best position in which to set up an ambush for anyone travelling through the pass from the direction of the faerie realm. They chose two ledges directly opposite each other, about twelve feet above the track. The rocks sloped downwards and provided the perfect spot to surprise an enemy from above and to quickly push home any attack.

Now in position, Slimonica split up her small group, two on one side, herself and the third nun on the other. She'd had the blades of the swords and daggers and the tips of the arrows dipped in a black dye in order to prevent any light glinting on their metal surfaces giving their position away. She had also given orders to paint the buckles of tunics and the bridles of the horses; Slimonica was taking no chances. They settled down to await the arrival of their prey, one slept while the other kept the first watch. Slimonica let her comrade sleep first. They had no idea how long they might have to wait, the longer the better she thought. She had things to think about.

Slimonica was ambitious. From the night she had deserted the graveyard, and ever since she was selected for the Cadaveran nuns, she had vowed she would rise as high as she could. She was determined to make a success of this second chance even though it was an evil one. When Morbidea's armies march through the Yett, taking the war to humankind, she would be at the forefront and she knew exactly where her revenge would lie.

She sat watching the approach, her thoughts drifting to her childhood. It was strange she no longer enjoyed the heat and warmth of the sun, remembering how as a child she loved lying in the summer meadow picking daisies to make chains, holding them up to the light and delighting in her mother's smile when she took them home.

'Monica, they are beautiful,' her mother would beam.

Monica's mother and father had wanted more for her. They had secured her a place as a servant girl in The Big House, owned by the local magistrate and Member of Parliament. On her first day she was met by the housekeeper Miss Flint, a twisted and sour woman who marched her to a sparse little room and explained her duties. Miss Flint walked quickly despite needing the aid of a stick. Her blackthorn cane was gnarled and hard. A carved brass bloodhound's head formed the handle.

'Know your place and speak only when spoken to. I will be watching you, my girl,' she told Monica her granite face so close that spittle landed in the child's eyes.

That night Monica silently sobbed herself to sleep, missing the warmth and love of her family. A week later, tired from endless hours of work she knelt to pray by her bedside. She prayed for strength and to be forgiven for the thoughts she had harboured against Miss Flint.

'Amen.'

Before climbing into bed Monica picked up the hard pillow in an attempt to fluff it up. In the candlelight a shimmer caught her eye. A gold and diamond brooch was lying where the pillow had been. Monica picked up the brooch utterly bemused by its presence when the door swiftly opened and Miss Flint limped into the room.

'Caught you nicely, haven't I?' the words grinding out from greying teeth. Behind her in the hall another of the young maids stood frightened, wringing her hands. 'Fetch the master.' The girl scurried off. Monica tried to gather her thoughts. 'We won't put up with thieves in this house,' she grabbed Monica by the upper arm and dug her thumb into the flesh. You're for it now, my girl.' Miss Flint pushed Monica hard against the small washstand causing a jug of water to spill across the floor.

'I didn't. . . I found it under my pillow,' Monica stuttered, trying to make sense of what was happening.

'You're a lying little thief,' spat Miss Flint. 'I am going to beat some decency into you.'

She advanced toward Monica with her cane raised, ready to bring the brass head down onto Monica's shoulders when suddenly she slipped and slammed backwards onto the wet floor. Her head whacked off the wooden end of the bed and she lay there motionless as a widening pool of blood poured from the gaping wound. The cane lay across her face, the brass head touching the floor, the bloodhound seeming to lap up her blood. Monica was terrified.

'Miss Flint! Miss Flint.'

She knelt down beside her, where just a moment before she had knelt to pray. Picking up the cane, drops of blood from the dog's mouth dripped across Flint's white face.

'Please! Miss Flint, please wake up.'

The stone-grey eyes stared at the ceiling. When the master of the house entered the room he found Monica leaning over Miss Flint, the bloodied cane in one hand and the stolen brooch in the other.

Monica was charged with theft and murder. A week later, at the age of sixteen, she was publicly hanged. Her mother and father were made to watch.

A shadow flashed across Slimonica's mind, shaking her from her reverie. She had much to avenge. That old crone, Flint, died too easily, she thought to herself. I would have made her suffer a thousand deaths but I will get the master and his family. They will pay for what they did. A sound like the clink from a bridle instantly brought her from her thoughts.

She kicked the boot of her sleeping partner who woke to see Slimonica with a warning finger to her lips. Firing an arrow across the canyon to alert her companions, they immediately grabbed their weapons. Slimonica pointed up the pass and all four crouched in readiness for the ambush.

A shadow, swift as an arrow, shot across the walls of the canyon as Mouldy sped on his newly-spread hawks wings. He banked and descended to the spot where Malcolm was mounted on Meg. Swooping and arresting his velocity, he landed with effortless grace on Malcolm's outstretched glove.

'One thing I'll say for these hawks is that they can fairly travel at speed.'

'Did you see anything?' asked Malcolm.

'Four Cadaverans, armed and ready to ambush us further along the canyon.'

'Cadaverans. We will have to be on our guard. Even though I outrank them they are known to be immune to the authority of the regular army. They have been suspected of killing officers rather than obeying their command.'

'What should we do?' questioned Meg.

'We will stick to the story. If they believe it, fine, if not I shall have a fight on my hands. Whatever happens I want you and Mouldy to get away as quickly as you can. They will not think it strange for a horse to bolt or a hawk to fly off in the midst of a fight. That way you can both keep the rendezvous.'

'You expect us to run off and leave you. I can land a few kicks and I expect Mouldy could have an eye out with those claws of his.'

'That is very kind of you, but the important thing is for as many of us as possible to meet up with the children.'

'I think,' put in Mouldy, 'that we are in a situation where the outcome cannot be predicted. We should probably let events play out and see what happens.'

With the acceptance of this statement the trio continued along the pass, Malcolm began singing a soldier's song in his best carefree voice.

Slimonica and her troopers were positioned on the sloping rocks. Malcolm's singing grew louder. As he reached them he continued the song looking straight up at the Cadaverans as though they were his audience then, finishing, he took a small bow from his saddle.

'Good day, comrades,' he beamed, despite the drawn swords and bows which were pointed at him.

'Who are you and what brings you through this pass?' snapped Slimonica.

'Is it not obvious who I am? I am a commander in the forces of General MacMorna. As to why I am here, that is none of your business. Now, lower your bows and let me pass.'

'If you are one of the general's commanders, why are you travelling from the realm of the faerie queen, a known enemy of *our* people?'

Slimonica's stress on the word 'our' was a subtle trap. No person in the realm, especially those in the army, regarded the Cadaverans as part of their society. They were interlopers, undead creatures, only just tolerated and utterly despised. Malcolm could not ignore this or they would become more suspicious than they already were.

'Our people,' he repeated, feigning amusement. 'There are many enemies of *our* people.'

'Really.' replied Slimonica. 'And who might they be?'

'All who oppose Morbidea, our queen,' Malcolm answered with a charming smile causing the Cadaverans to become angry. One with a scar on her left cheek gripped her sword and looked ready to leap from the rock.

Meg shifted under him. Malcolm sensed her unease and took the initiative.

'If we are finished here, I have important information for General MacMorna.'

'We are not finished yet, commander. We have been tasked with finding a group that plan to enter the realm and create trouble for our queen. Among them are two children. We believe they are receiving help from the faerie people and expect them to travel this way.'

'Then I will be on my way and leave you and your warriors to the dangerous task of arresting small children,' replied Malcolm. The Cadaverans growled at the insult.

Leaning forward in his saddle, Malcolm added, 'Obviously there are no children here. I travel alone, as you can see.'

'Alone and from the land of our foes. You could be a spy and we would be failing in our duty if we did not interrogate you.'

Malcolm suspected the worst and sensed that they wanted to kill him. They would never dare execute an army commander in their own land. Here, however, far from the authority of the army they could dispose of him and get away with it. There would be no witnesses and it would gain them great praise in the ranks of their infernal sisterhood. It was time to pull rank.

'A spy? I have had enough of this idiocy. I will be on my way. If you impede my journey, believe me the general will hear of it.'

'The general will hear of nothing,' replied Slimonica. 'Hackscar here is itching to kill you. Aren't you Hackscar?'

The scarred Cadaveran smiled, showing a froth-corrupted mouth and teeth like ancient broken gravestones. Running down the sloping rock she leapt to the ground barring Malcolm's path.

'This is treason. You will be hanged for this, all of you.'

'That holds no fear for us. We have all been hanged before, master commander.' The Cadaverans laughed heartily at Slimonica's joke. 'Besides, one commander less will make it easier when we take over the army.'

Malcolm dismounted, put Mouldy onto the pummel of the saddle and drawing his sword walked confidently toward Hackscar who was grinning as if Christmas had come and Malcolm was the turkey.

'You have one last chance to save your scrawny Cadaveran necks. Stand aside and let me pass.'

Almost before he had finished, Hackscar lurched forward with a thrust to Malcolm's chest which he hurriedly but effectively parried. Balancing his blade in his hand he waited, assessing his opponent's skill. Another charging run threatened a direct cut down upon his head which he blocked, stepping swiftly aside as Hackscar lumbered past. Malcolm deduced that there was no finesse in Hackscar's swordplay. She relied on brute strength, yelling each time she attacked to frighten her opponent. She came on again, her sword aiming to run through Malcolm's abdomen. Malcolm stepped into the attack turning slightly, safely deflecting the thrust, hitting Hackscar in the face with the hilt of his sword as her momentum carried her past. Malcolm jumped lightly back putting some distance between them to prepare for her next attack. He did not have long to wait. Enraged by the hit to her face, Hackscar gripped her sword and charged at Malcolm with all the fury she could muster. This time Malcolm did not stand his ground. Meg and Mouldy were surprised to see that he too had gone on the attack and was racing towards Hackscar. Seconds before they clashed Malcolm dived at the ground, executing a perfect forward roll. The momentum carried him onto his feet under Hackscar's sword tip and as he rose he thrust the point of his blade up through Hackscar's neck with such force that it went in up to the hilt. Malcolm pushed her backwards and pulled his sword from her neck. The black blood poured from the wound as she buckled, crumpled to her knees and, with a look of disbelief, fell forward into the dirt to begin her journey to hell.

Slimonica and the others were momentarily stunned.

'He's mine!' cried the other sword-wielding Cadaveran, running down the sloping rock and leaping nimbly to engage Malcolm. She circled carefully before launching a sustained and accomplished set of thrusts and cuts. Malcolm knew he was facing an opponent experienced in the art of fencing. As they fought it was apparent that they were evenly matched. They cut and thrust, each trying to find an advantage. The Cadaveran's precise swordplay soon caused Malcolm to tire. He dodged a cut to his head but was slashed across the shoulder. He winced and felt blood run down his arm. Luckily it was not his sword arm but he was now at a serious disadvantage. He staggered backwards close to the wall of the canyon with the

Cadaveran following, sensing she had the upper hand. Malcolm made a feeble thrust to her left shoulder which she parried fiercely, causing him to spin in a half turn and hit the rock face. He clung there, his sword arm limp, the weapon trailing on the ground. He was beaten. The Cadaveran lunged to run her sword through his back. Malcolm timed his move perfectly. He lunged to the right and the Cadaveran's sword point jarred into the rock face as he spun with a backhanded swipe that cut her head clean from her shoulders. Malcolm leaned against the rock breathing heavily, tired and wounded. He still had another two of the devils to cope with.

'Enough!' cried Slimonica. 'Finish him with an arrow.'

The last of Slimonica's troopers raised her bow and let fly an arrow straight at Malcolm's heart. Like a flash Mouldy launched from the saddle and streaked toward Malcolm intercepting the missile and catching the shaft in his beak. It was a short reprieve. Slimonica and her comrade reloaded their bows.

'Shoot the bird!' she yelled. 'I'll kill. . .' The arrow pierced her throat and cut off her final words. Slimonica fell on her knees and, knowing the fate that awaited her, pitched forward to die. A second arrow sealed the fate of the last Cadaveran. All four were dead. Behind them stood Eilean and Heather, they had reached the pass and come up behind the Cadaverans who were too busy with Malcolm to notice them. Heather had loosed the two swift arrows that had saved Malcolm's life.

Meg trotted over to Malcolm. 'Are you alright?'

'Fine, it's just a bit of a cut on my shoulder.'

'Who are they?' questioned Meg as the two girls approached.

'They are officers of the general's guard, by the looks of it. We are not out of the woods yet.'

'Or the canyon,' quipped Meg.

'Why is it we always have to dig you out of a scrape, Malcolm? You can't be left on your own for five minutes.'

Malcolm was utterly astounded. 'Eilean! I . . . I . . .'

'Close your mouth, Malcolm, you'll catch flies in this heat!'

'I can't believe it's you! And Heather! Thank goodness you are both safe. What has been happening? Why are you dressed like this?'

'We could ask you the same question, commander!'

They made their way back to where the girls had left their horses. Sitting for a while they ate some rations and related their tales to one another. Heather treated Malcolm's wound with a soothing balm and bound it with gauze.

'It should heal quickly.' she said. 'It has not gone to the bone.'

'I made it seem worse than it was to get the better of that Cadaveran fiend. She was good with that sword.'

'Not good enough though,' laughed Eilean. 'You made short work of those two.'

'The others would have had me if you had not appeared. I am glad you were able to make your escape, for my sake as well as yours. Tell me how you managed it.'

Malcolm was impressed by the manner in which the girls had made their escape but was saddened to hear that Paul had visited them. It confirmed what his Leachim thoughts suspected, that Paul was indeed the spy and in Morbidea's employ. He had the unenviable task of describing to Eilean the curse that had been put on her clan, the arrest and imprisonment of her brother and his fears of Paul's treachery.

'This is awful. For my father to arrest Callum and for Paul to betray his people, these are things unheard of in the history of our clan. How can the curse be broken?'

'Only Morbidea knows. She is the one who put this spell upon them. Only she can lift it.'

'None of us here are what we seem,' interrupted Heather. 'The hawk is an owl, Meg is no longer a grey mare and we, thanks to luck and cunning appear to be senior officers in Morbidea's army. But where are the children of the blood?'

'They travel separately across an underground lake, a plan to make our group less conspicuous. They are guided by Oxterguff, the queen's piper. We are to meet with them on the other side of the mountains.'

'Then Eilean and I must travel with you, Malcolm. We must help you regain the tail before Morbidea uses it to destroy our worlds,' said Heather.

'Heather is right and we must find a way to break this hideous curse,' said Eilean.

They mounted up and the band of friends began their journey north through the pass to the rendezvous with the children.

Chapter 18

QUILL CAVERN

Oxterguff pushed hard against the prow of the rowing boat. As the keel scraped from the shingle at the edge of the lake, the ink-black water lapped and wrapped around the hull; the boat became buoyant. Oxterguff pulled himself up and over the side then lit the lanterns at either end of the boat. Fiona dipped and pulled on the oars as they set out across the dark surface of the water into the unseen vastness of the subterranean cavern.

'Try to row gently,' advised Oxterguff. 'I doubt Morbidea's spies will be in this place but it's better to be on the side of caution.'

The group fell silent, their alerted senses straining for any hint of danger. Fiona had never rowed a boat before yet seemed to have a natural ability, dipping the oars without splashing and pulling back on the shafts with only the slightest of creaks from the rowlocks. The yellow glow from the lanterns created a shimmering halo around the boat before being swallowed up by the dark blackness of the water. Kirsty gave the tiniest of whimpers. Being afloat was not her most favourite environment; she much preferred solid ground.

After a few minutes, Oxterguff indicated to Fiona to stop rowing.

'We need to set our direction, if we keep rowing in the dark we could end up going round in circles.'

'How do we know which way to go?' Fiona asked.

Oxterguff's eyes sparkled in the lantern light and a mischievous grin played on his face as he gently extracted a large puddock from his satchel. Kirsty stretched forward for an enquiring sniff and the puddock let fly with one of his hind legs, slapping Kirsty's nose. She snorted and shook her head.

'Sorry about that, lass', Oxterguff scratched the dog's ear. 'He can be a wee bit bad-tempered at times'.

Fiona took a hold of Oxterguff's arm. 'How on earth can a frog help us find the right direction?'

'Simple really,' smiled Oxterguff, 'Purdy here is a navigational puddock. The queen has given him the coordinates for our journey.' Oxterguff put Purdy on the small bench seat and the beast shuffled into position.

'Five degrees left rudder and row straight ahead nor', nor' east,' gurgled Purdy.

'Now I've seen everything.' gasped Finn. 'We're heading for the realm of an evil witch with a wee fat puddock to show us the way. You couldn't make this up.'

'Mind your manners, ya cheeky wee poddil,' croaked Purdy, 'or you can get oot an' swim.'

'I see what you mean about his bad temper,' said Finn.

Oxterguff pointed into the darkness. 'Five degrees left rudder, straight ahead nor, nor east,' confirmed Oxterguff.

Fiona began rowing as Oxterguff adjusted the rudder and the little crew continued on, the gentle lapping of the water at odds with the trepidation in the hearts of the boat's occupants.

After some time Fiona was beginning to tire. She and Oxterguff carefully swapped places making as little movement as possible as they did so.

'I'm starving, I would eat that puddock's legs if we didn't need him to show us the way,' Finn announced.

'We should reach the opposite shore in a few more hours.' assured Oxterguff. 'We can look for food then.'

'Two hours?' rasped Finn. 'I'll never last that long.'

'You'll just have to!' snapped Fiona. 'Now please be quiet and stop making a fuss about food.'

Finn sat back in a huff with his arms folded and a scowl on his somewhat grubby face. He stared at the water not wanting to make eye contact with any of the others. It was just then that something caught his eye. An object bobbed up from below the surface of the water and floated along beside the boat. Finn could not believe what he was looking at. He blinked once, then again, and it was still there. It was an apple, glistening in the dark water, tantalisingly red and appetising. Finn's stomach rumbled as another apple broke the surface then another and another. He glanced quickly at the others but none of them seemed to have noticed. Sneakily, he placed his cupped hand into the water and began to paddle it towards the boat causing the apple to be drawn nearer to his grasp. His blue eyes gleamed and his mouth watered as the succulent red of the apple's skin tempted him.

'Look, apples,' he called out, as he plucked one from the surface. 'Pull your hand through the water and you'll get one; it's easier than dooking.' He lifted the apple and opened his mouth for a generous bite.

Oxterguff, who had been studying a map and drawing up plans in his head spun round as the words registered in his head.

'FINN NO!' Oxterguff lunged for Finn but it was too late.

The boy's teeth sank deep tearing off a large mouthful along with a sharp barbed hook. Finn's head jerked back as he squealed in pain. He felt a sharp tug as the hook pulled down behind his teeth and pushed out through his lower jaw. His panic escalated as he realised he was being pulled forcibly towards the edge of the boat. He noticed the water quivering where a barely discernible line tugged from beneath the surface. Oxterguff seeing the line drew his dirk and moved swiftly but he was not quick enough.

'Fiona!' Finn squealed as a strong tug from the line jerked his head pulling him entirely out of the boat into the black water. There was a momentary splash. Finn disappeared.

Barking, Kirsty leapt from the boat and doggy-paddled over towards the radiating ripples of water where Finn went down. She swam around in circles whimpering and biting at the water expecting him to resurface so that she could pull him to the safety of the boat.

As Finn's body was wrenched from the boat he instinctively inhaled a last breath. He twisted and turned, fighting against the hook and line. The light from the boat's lanterns began fading as he was drawn deeper into the cold inky water. Fear tore at his heart. He knew his last breath was running out. He remembered talking to Fiona in bed one night about how there had to be a last time for everything. He thought of the last time he had played with Kirsty, the last time he had galloped across the field on Meg's back and the last time he had seen his father. Lots of last times flooded through his mind as he was drawn further and further away from those he loved and the world where he lived. He recalled the last time his mother had smiled at him and was aware that he was no longer struggling. His body had become calm and his fear had gone. It was as if he was resigned to his fate. Even the pain in his jaw had subsided slightly.

A sharp, barbed and jaggy grip around his neck shook him from his final thoughts and alerted him of his situation once more. He struggled fiercely. Another scraping grip held his ankles and then his wrists. Finn was terrified and aware that his lungs were near to bursting. He desperately wanted to open his mouth and breathe. Lights danced in front of his face, shapes moved about him and he could hear underwater voices.

'Hold it tight.'

'Don't let it squirm.'

The scratching at his neck stopped but was quickly replaced when his head was gripped by what felt like jaggy-nettled fingers on his face. Without warning the hook in his mouth was pulled free, the pain causing him to yelp and let out the last of the air in his lungs.

He was exhausted. He needed to inhale.

'Stick it in the keep-bubble,' a voice commanded.

More of the scratching pulled at his limbs as he was thrust forward. Finn inhaled deeply expecting water to rush into his lungs. Instead he received a large dose of life sustaining air. He gulped the air deeply again and again gasping until his breathing reached some kind of equilibrium and he was able to take stock of his predicament. He was deep below the surface of the lake but inside a large spherical bubble, big enough to hold four or five Finn-sized people. It should have been quite comfortable as it enveloped, supported and floated gently near the bottom of the lake. In these circumstances, however, it was not comfortable. Finn's face and neck were scratched as were his wrists and ankles. The blood from his jaw was still trickling onto his shirt and he suddenly realised how cold he was. The only consolation was that he was alive and breathing.

'It's a beauty, Molak,' announced a voice as a light moved closer to the bubble.

'Let me see it,' said another.

'It was me that caught it,' came from a third.

From inside the bubble Finn saw a strange creature staring in at him. It had large cloudy eyes either side of a huge head from the centre of which extended a long antenna with a light on the end. The light illuminated the bubble, allowing the creature to inspect Finn. Two more lights approached from behind the creature, bathing it in a glow that enabled Finn to get a better look at his main observer. It was some kind of gross, hideous fish, more stumpy than long with the head making up about half the size of its body. Its fins resembled bats wings with long, thin, stick-like fingers, sharp, hooked and bony. Finn guessed that it was those fins which had held and scratched him. All three aquatic creatures now stared intently into the keep-bubble, the light from their antennae highlighting their grotesque features. Grey pockmarked skin covered their heads and body and large ovoid eyes sat like mercury lakes in a lunar landscape.

'Racu's asking, what is it?' enquired the one in the middle.

'Podrak doesn't know. Podrak's never seen anything like it,' replied the fish creature on the left.

Their voices drooled heavily and Finn noticed that their large lips, which were drawn back over massive human-like teeth, hardly moved as they spoke.

'Podrak's thinking it is ugly, whatever it is. Do you think it's safe to eat it?' Finn did not like the sound of that question.

'Racu's thinking if we boil it in a stew it should be safe to eat.' Racu's fish stomach rumbled at the thought of a stew and a bubble of air escaped from his mouth and slipped away to the surface.

'Podrak's asking, what thinks you Molak, you're the one that catched it?'

'Molak is very excited. My could be famous. No pacu fish has ever caught anything like this before.'

'Racu's thinking we should bash it on the head and put it in a stew,' said Racu, his gastric juices influencing his thinking.

'Podrak's asking is it maybe poisonous?'

'Molak owns it, it was my that catched it,' drooled Molac. 'Molac will decide what to do with it. Bash it, eat it or keep it.'

Finn lurched forward and screamed, 'Leave me alone.'

The three lights on the antennae suddenly went out and Finn found himself in complete darkness, alone and frightened.

'No, don't go away,' he pleaded. 'Where are you? Come back.' There was nothing but absolute silence and utter darkness. He curled up in his bubble and started to cry. 'I want my sister,' he whimpered, 'I want Fiona.'

A tiny voice came from out of the dark. 'My nearly squirted myself when it shouted,' whispered Molak. 'My didn't think it had speaks. It's saying it wants a Fiona.'

'Podrak's asking, what's a Fiona?'

'Racu's thinking it's dangerous. We should burst its bubble, drown it and eat it.'

'I can hear you whispering out there, I'm not deaf you know.'

There was a momentary silence as one by one the three antennae lit up again. Podrak, Racu and Molak swam back into place outside Finn's bubble, their scratchy, jaggy fins moving gently to keep them in position.

'You there, thing in keep-bubble, what is it you are?' Molac cautiously enquired.

'Yes thing, what is it you are?' echoed Podrak.

'Come on, speak thing, speak,' drooled Racu.

'I'm a boy, do you understand. I'm just a boy!'

'Thing says its name is Justaboy,' repeated Molac.

'No! I didn't. I'm just... My name is Finn. Why have you got me in here?'

'You bited the apple.'

'You took the hook,' said Molac

Finn was finding it hard to work out which fish was doing the talking as their lips gave away little. 'You put a hook in an apple. What a stupid, dangerous thing to do. Why did you do that?'

'So we can catch things like you.'

Finn was exasperated. 'Look, I can't tell which of you is speaking. Why don't you put your lights out and only put them on when you are talking?'

'The thing, Finn, wants only light when speaks are coming,' Molac explained to the others.

'No, we need lights for seeing you thing, Finn. But we can be flashing light when we have speaks. Then you can tell if the speaks come from Molac, Podrak or Racu,' suggested Racu.

'Good,' said Finn, 'that's even better. Molac, if you are the one who caught me, you speak first.'

Molac's antenna light remained steady for a few moments then it flashed. 'My wants to know what you are is, thing Finn? Molac has not seen a thing Finn before.'

'Finn, my name is Finn and I am not a thing. I am a human, a boy human.'

'A human?' flashed Molac. 'What is be that?'

Finn was finding it hard to explain in a way they would understand.

'I'm not a fish, I don't live in water. I come from above the surface, from a land far away.' Suddenly all their lights began flashing. Finn suspected that his words had caused them some alarm.

'Racu thinks we is be in big trouble,' flashed Racu.

Podrak was so excited he spoke without flashing. 'We must not have speaks with anyone about this. We is not allowed to take things from surface.'

'Promise you will not tell, human Finn. Our trouble would be much more than not small,' flashed Molac.

'My thinks we should get rid of it,' flashed Racu. 'We could bash it and hide it.'

'No!' cried Podrak with a nervous flash. 'We get in huge, bigger trouble. My thinks we should tell and say accident or big mistake. We could do pretend sorry.'

'There is another way,' shouted Finn. The three guilty fish stopped talking and listened intently to what he had to say.

'You could just release the bubble and let me float to the surface.' Finn had thought this might be his best option. Even floating on the surface would be better than being down here where at any moment the option of bashing and stewing might be revisited.

'But he is mine. My catched him. My could just keep him and not have speaks with anyone about him. My could keep him in the bubble and only show him to my best friends. My could feed him nice worms and keep him forever until he dies, then bury him under the rocks. No one would know.'

'No! That's a bad idea.' cried Finn. 'You'll get caught. Someone would tell on you.' The thought of being in the bubble forever eating only worms had scared him badly, just when he thought he might persuade them to let him go.

'That's a good idea,' said Racu. 'My thinks you could show him to people. You could charge them five worms to look at him. It not cost you anything to feed him then.'

All of a sudden they were surrounded by an alarming noise. 'Whooo, whooo, whooo.'

Long, slender silver fish appeared from all directions. They moved at great speed, a thin blue neon stripe along their sides flashing in the dark. They surrounded the keep bubble and the pacu fish, the blue neon flashing brightly in the darkness as they rocked in the water, stern expressions on their faces. The pacu fish were stricken with fear. One of the silver fish glided up. Finn noticed three white stripes on its fins.

'Hello, hello, hello! What have we got here? You three, I might have known it, caught red-finned! What will your mothers have to say? Poaching rare species from the surface by the looks of things, well you're for it now. You'll be swimming in the school for bad fish.'

Podrak squirted himself and began to whimper. Molak and Raku quivered. Finn felt he had to try and help even though they had threatened to bash, drown and stew him.

'Excuse me sir!' cried Finn, peering from the keep-bubble. 'It's not really their fault. They found me in this bubble and were trying to get it loose so I could float back to the surface and find my friends.' Finn hated telling this lie but thought that if he could get the pacu fish out of trouble he might have some sort of chance.

'What is your name?' the striped fish asked.

'Finn, sir, I'm just a wee laddie,' replied Finn pathetically.

'Right, wee laddie, I can tell from the mess of your jaw and the scratch marks on your neck that these three poached you from the surface. Now I want you to tell me the truth.'

Finn had no option so he told the whole story to which all present listened intently.

'Which way was your boat heading?' asked the fish in charge.

'I don't know. We were being guided by a puddock.'

Another fish zoomed up. 'One of the wee fry has reported a boat heading for the shore under the mountain. They reckon it will reach the beach in a couple of hours.'

'Get Tully and Allen to free the laddie's keep-bubble. They can tow him to the shore. When you get ashore, laddie, you'll find dry twigs and branches, there is also plenty of flint. I suggest you make a fire, get your clothes dried and get yourself warmed up. Your boat won't be far behind.' He turned to the pacu fish. 'You three come here.' The trembling delinquents did as they were told. 'From what we hear, the world above the cavern is in a bad way. This laddie is an endangered species and you took him from the surface. We're going to put him back and if I ever catch you three at this again you'll be for it. Got it?'

'Yes! Molak is very sorry.'

'Racu too is sorry we catched you.'

'So too is Podrak and it is not a pretend sorry.'

'Right, let's go see your parents. We'll see what they have to say about your shenanigans. He led the culprits off to face the consequences of what they had done while Tully and Allen tackled the keep-bubble. Biting through the fronds, they freed it from its anchorage. They made off towing the bubble and flashed through the water at great speed, their blue neon lights clearing a path ahead of them.

Finn lay back in the bubble and now that the danger and fear had left him, he realised just how much his jaw ached. His clothes were soaked with water and blood. He pulled his shirt sleeve over his fist and held it under his jaw, stemming any flow of blood that might still be oozing from the wound.

Despite the cold and the pain Finn felt a thrill of excitement. He was amazed at the speed with which his two fishy saviours could flash through the depths. The bubble was comfortable and the 'Whooo, whooo, whooo' sound of their movement was quite hypnotic.

It did not take long to reach the shore. The bubble slowed and then broke the surface of the water. Tully and Allen dropped the fronds and nudged Finn closer to the shore then they tore at the bubble with their teeth until it burst. Finn pulled himself free and waded ashore.

'Right, laddie,' said Tully in a warm and friendly manner, 'we'll stay at the edge here until you get your fire going, then we need to get back.'

'Thank you,' Finn started to collect kindling and found lots of dry straw among the rocks. He was glad of the light from his fishy guardians. It didn't take him long to get his fire going.

'I think it is safe enough to leave you now,' chuckled Allen. 'You made a good job of that fire and your friends should be along very soon. Good luck.'

'Thank you, you've saved my life.'

The two fish turned and slipped below the surface of the water. As they sped back to join their shoal Allen chuckled again. 'It's nice to see creatures released back to their proper environment.'

'I know,' replied Tully. 'It really makes the job worthwhile.'

Finn decided to make four fires and soon sat in the middle of them, steam rising from his clothes as they began to dry out. As the heat seeped back into his bones he became warm enough to take off his shirt and hang it from some sticks nearer to the fire. Soon he was warm enough to do the same with his boots, socks and trousers. The wound in his jaw did not feel as big as he thought it would be. It must have been a fine hook that was used to bait the apple. It did, however, nip and ache, enough to remind him of his adventure.

He began re-living the entire event. He knew he had never been so scared or felt so alone. He'd really believed he was going to die and would never see Fiona or his mum again. Finn started to laugh remembering what Molak, or was it Racu or Podrak had said. 'What's a Fiona?' The more he thought of it the harder he laughed. He laughed until his sides hurt. 'What's a Fiona?' Who could answer that? Whatever Fiona was, she was getting the biggest brother cuddle of her life when she got off that boat.

Chapter 19

RETURN FROM THE DEPTHS

Oxterguff kept the boat positioned for a long time over the spot where Finn had gone overboard. Eventually, when it became apparent that the boy had not survived he decided they would have to carry on. It was with a sad and heavy heart that he pulled away. He had not known Finn long but he had taken a liking to the lad. This was a tragic incident and a bad omen.

Fiona sat at the back of the boat sobbing, her hands folded in her lap, rocking back and forth. Kirsty lay at her feet whimpering, wet fur soaking into the planks of the boat. Fiona could not believe that Finn was gone. Thoughts flew through her mind. Finn had not wanted to come on this quest, it was her fault that he had drowned. How will I be able to carry on without him she thought? How can there be a world without Finn?

They rowed on in shock, nursing their own sorrow, each stroke of the oars taking them further away from Finn. The silence was punctuated only by Purdy's orders to change direction. Fiona pulled a handkerchief from her pocket and blew her nose then used the corner to wipe tears from her eyes. Through her blinks she saw lights on the horizon.

'Look, Guffy, what's that?'

Oxterguff turned in his seat and stretching forward put out the lamp at the prow. 'Put the stern lamp out, Fiona. We must be careful. Maybe Morbidea has discovered our plan and sent troops to capture us.'

Oxterguff rowed slowly and silently toward the light. He put Purdy back in the satchel and brought the boat to a halt when he could see more clearly. He counted four fires. 'It could be a camp,' he whispered.

They both peered from the darkness to see what awaited them. The camp appeared to be empty. They rowed in cautiously until the boat grounded on the shore.

Oxterguff pulled the boat up on the shingle and was helping Fiona out when a familiar voice called, 'About time, what kept you?'

Finn walked from the shadows into the firelight. Kirsty gave a yelp of joy, bolted over to Finn jumping excitedly all round him. The others just stood, registering who was standing in front of them.

'Finn!' screamed Fiona, running to him, laughing and crying at the same time. They grabbed each other tightly while Oxterguff stood smiling in bewilderment; Kirsty was on her hind legs trying to join the crushing cuddle.

Fiona was sobbing with joy, 'Oh Finn, Finn. How did you. . . ? What. . . ? How did you get here? We thought you were dead, drowned out there.'

'I nearly was. I thought I was done for. Okay, you can stop now. You're squeezing too tight.'

'I thought I was never going to see you again.'

'I know, me too.' And he gave his sister the tightest cuddle even though he'd just asked her to stop.

'You certainly gave us a fright, laddie. We waited ages but thought we'd lost you. So what happened?'

'Wait 'til I tell you, you'll never believe it.' They sat by the fires, watching Finn's animated face as he retold his incredible adventure.

'That is a fascinating tale, laddie. There's so much we don't know about what dwells below the lake but you've certainly added to our knowledge. For now, however, we should be getting on our way. I dare say you need something to eat.' It was then they realised that they were all very hungry. Fiona and Finn looked at one another.

'Not apples!' they chorused.

'I could go a juicy worm,' laughed Finn.

They pulled the boat ashore and hid it among the rocks. Using the lanterns they made their way along the path from the shore.

'This path will lead us out from under the mountain. It will be good to get into the light again. It surprises me that anything can live down here.'

'I'm not surprised you don't like it compared to the beauty of the faerie realm,' said Fiona.

'It is a bonny world right enough,' replied Oxterguff proudly. 'Hang onto those thoughts when we set foot in Morbidea's realm, beautiful it is not. The best thing about it will be the journey home.'

Oxterguff was right. As they emerged from a cave on the side of the mountain the land that awaited them was a dour and desolate place. Sloping away from the dull scree of the mountain was a world devoid of colour. The hazy sun dappled a grey light over the land; nature looked withered.

'It looks like a land where orphans might live,' mused Finn.

'What do you mean?' said Fiona.

'It looks unhappy. Orphans are always unhappy aren't they? It looks like a place where they might live,' said Finn.

Fiona did not respond. She knew Finn's mind worked differently from other people but she sort of understood what he was getting at.

'Whatever it is, bairns, it's a land we must travel through. Morbidea's castle is far to the north so we must journey on. Stay on your guard, Morbidea's troops will be searching for us and who knows what creatures lurk in those woods.'

'Any good news?' asked Finn.

Oxterguff laughed. 'Of course, the good news is we have made it this far. Now we must continue in order to keep our rendezvous with the others. If they too have made it, we are to meet them at The Temple of the Dead.'

'Oh goody, that sounds like fun,' said Finn. 'We couldn't meet them somewhere like the Temple of the Happy could we? Guess not.' Finn answered himself as he set off down the mountain slope, Fiona and Oxterguff following behind.

Ahead of them, Malcolm and the others, having survived Antler's Pass, had already made their way safely across the open scrubland and reached the forest beyond.

Chapter 20

WHAT THE DRACOSCOPE SAW

Oxterguff and the children descended the scree-covered slopes before reaching the level ground on the northern side of Antler Pass. It was not easy to keep their footing and they slipped several times along the way, scraping their legs and raising clouds of dust in the process. Even Kirsty wasn't as sure-footed as usual. Oxterguff worried that their exposed position would give them away or cause suspicion among anyone who spotted them.

By the time Finn, Fiona, Oxterguff and Kirsty had reached the foot of the mountain they were filthy, covered in dust and very thirsty. They sat on a large boulder to briefly rest and catch their breath. Oxterguff produced a small flask of water from his satchel and they drank what was left, Fiona pouring some into Finn's cupped hands for Kirsty to get a share.

'We must go,' said Oxterguff as he scanned the horizon. 'I don't like being out in the open like this.'

They gathered themselves, dusted down their clothing and set off across the flat plain. High above them, circling silently on expansive wings, soared a dracoscope; a large bird-like creature with one eye in the centre of its head. This telescopic eye zoomed in and locked onto the children. The dracoscope was one of Morbidea's many pets and what the dracoscope saw, Morbidea saw.

Far to the north, in the utmost tower of Raven's Neuk, Morbidea stood motionless. Perched in front of her was the dracoscope's chick. Morbidea watched the chick's enormous eye intently.

Smiling, she said, 'There you are my sweeties,' as she watched Finn and Fiona cross the curved screen of the chick's eye. Beside her stood Stinkeye with a bewildered expression on her face. She could not understand how two stupid children and a strange faerie type had eluded Slimonica and her Cadaveran comrades.

'You told me you were sending your swiftest Cadaverans to capture these children. It appears you have failed me, Stinkeye.'

'I sent Slimonica, she is one of my best.'

'I know of Slimonica; she has shown great promise.' She scratched the chick at the back of the ear with a long slender finger. 'Listen, precious chick, tell mummy to fly over Antler Pass, I want to see what's there.' The chick closed its eye and when it opened again the image swept the length of the pass, cleared the mountains and entered the air space above the faerie realm. There, the dracoscope banked and swept back along the pass, side slipping as it soared.

Morbidea and Stinkeye peered into the chick's eye, eagerly searching for some sign of what had happened. Then it became clear. The bodies of the Cadaverans lay where they had fallen. The dracoscope zoomed in to register on the individual Cadaverans. Morbidea grabbed the chick by the neck. It squawked a startled squawk. 'Tell Mummy to come home.' She let the chick go and swept across the room to stand in front of an ancient fireplace. The flames roared as she approached. Stinkeye followed nervously, aware she could be in big trouble. She thought it best not to speak first. Morbidea was seething but when she turned she seemed to have composed herself.

'Those children and the faerie dwarf did not do this. They must have others helping them, others who know to shoot for the neck and cut for the head for it is the only way to kill my Cadaverans. Put all units on high alert. I want to know who they are, where they are. I want to know how many. I want them caught immediately, do you understand?'

'Yes, Majesty, we should redeploy the dracoscope.'

'There is no point. Once they make it into the forest she would not be able to see them. Besides I need her for other tasks. I want patrols out to cover the forest's edge. Use as many units as you need. As soon as they emerge from that forest I want them apprehended and brought here. I want the pleasure of killing those children myself. I cannot have them at liberty when the ceremony takes place.'

'Very good, Majesty,' Stinkeye stood awaiting further instructions.

Morbidea's calm evaporated. 'Well, don't stand there you fool.' Stinkeye saluted, turned for the door and quickly made her way down the staircase. She had only descended a few steps when Morbidea's voice caught up with her. 'Do not fail me again, Stinkeye, or you will regret the day I resurrected you.'

Chapter 21

TEMPLE OF THE DEAD

Kirsty was the first to reach the edge of the forest. She stopped and sniffed the air trying to gain some sort of intelligence as to what was ahead of them. She sensed something unwholesome about the place. Oxterguff and the children arrived by her side, glad to be clear of the scrubland.

Oxterguff took a deep breath. 'Let's go. Stick close together.' Kirsty whimpered and all three looked at her. Her tail was between her legs and her ears were drooped.

'She doesn't want to go in there,' said Finn.

'Who does?' added Fiona. 'It's not as if we have any choice.'

Taking this as a cue for action Oxterguff nodded and set off into the forest followed by the children. For the first time on the expedition Kirsty did not forge ahead. As they made their way through the dense stale forest, units of Stinkeye's Cadaverans were heading to patrol the forest's northern edges. Oxterguff used his sword to hack a path through the undergrowth as they walked. The air was filled with a cloying, putrid odour which stuck in their throats and nostrils. Kirsty sneezed and rubbed at her nose with the crook of her paw.

'This place stinks,' puffed Finn, 'and I'm sweating like a pig.'

'Nice image.' laughed Oxterguff. 'The undergrowth should thin out as we get further in.' A little further on Oxterguff was proved right. The vegetation thinned out and the going got easier. They soon connected with a well-worn path and the speed of their progress brightened their spirits. Kirsty's tail and ears had returned to normal and she was soon venturing ahead again to check out the terrain. They forged on making good progress.

Oxterguff stopped and took Purdy out of his satchel, placing him on a fallen tree trunk.

'What time of day is it?' he asked. The puddock shifted around in a circle, his tongue shooting in and out tasting the air.

'Just after midday,' croaked Purdy.

'Weather prediction?' asked Oxterguff. Again the puddock's tongue flicked.

'Heavy rain, very soon, most likely torrential,' informed the puddock. Suddenly a coordinated screech from the canopy above startled them. In a flash, a furry blur shot from the undergrowth, grabbed Purdy and disappeared down the path. By the time they realised what had happened all they saw was Kirsty barking and racing in pursuit of the puddock thief.

'What was that?' shouted Finn in alarm.

'I don't know, but whatever it is it's got our puddock,' cried Oxterguff. 'Come on, follow Kirsty.' They sped off along the path after Kirsty and the thief. As they ran sticks and stone-like fruits rained down upon them from the trees above. Finn caught one of the stony fruits firm in his palm. He reckoned it would have been pretty sore had it hit him. Suddenly, the path ended. They stopped.

In front of them towered the ruins of an ancient building, a vast vine-entwined temple. Vegetation crawled between the crumbling pillars devouring the stonework. Statues of once-revered figures stared majestically over the forest's canopy. Heads and arms of stone lay embedded in the ground, half buried. Amongst them was Kirsty, barking furiously at a cornered monkey-like creature cowering under a rock. It held the puddock in its grasp, screeching fiercely. A symphony of ear-piercing screeches descended from the trees and vines above. The frightened creature looked as if it might release the puddock but then screeched.

'Leave me. Leave me alone or I'll bite its head off.'

The cry was echoed by its friends high in the canopy. 'Bite its head off, bite it off.'

'Kirsty stop,' cried Fiona, 'can't you see it's scared.' Kirsty stopped barking but kept the beast cornered, giving a low growl to show her displeasure.

'We're not going to hurt you, but we need our puddock back,' said Fiona gently.

'I might eat it.' The monkey creature opened its mouth displaying a vicious set of teeth. Staring stubbornly at Kirsty it slowly lifted Purdy towards its gaping mouth. Without thinking, Finn launched the hard fruit. It was a swift shot and struck the creature right between the eyes causing the animal to drop the puddock. The monkey rolled backwards holding its head. Purdy leapt for the safety of Oxterguff's satchel as Kirsty raced in and grabbed the animal by the scruff of the neck. It hung limp from Kirsty's jaws.

'Uhya! My head, my head,' it moaned quietly.

The noise above them had ceased as the other members of the furry troupe peered down, fearing what might happen to their unfortunate companion.

'You'll have more to worry about than a sore head,' snapped Oxterguff. 'What are you playing at taking our puddock?'

'We just want to be left alone, leave the whilpets alone. We don't want you to kidnap us. We don't want to be prisoners of the queen.'

'What's it havering about?' asked Finn. 'I think that dunt on the head must have knocked it daft. And what's a whilpet?'

'What queen?' asked Fiona. 'Do you mean Morbidea?'

At the mention of that name the symphony of screeching began once more, striking anguish into the whole troupe.

'She's the evil one. Her soldiers steal whilpets and they are never heard of again. We want to stay here where whilpets belong.'

'We're not here to kidnap you,' cried Oxterguff somewhat annoyed. 'We are on a quest and the last thing we need is a bunch of stupid, screeching monkeys giving us away.'

'He's telling the truth,' Fiona said softly, trying to calm the whilpet. 'We are on a quest, one that will stop Morbidea becoming more powerful. A quest to prevent a great war of revenge, you have nothing to fear from us.'

'Then you may carry on your way,' rasped a deep voice from the darkness of the temple. The screeching stopped. An ancient, slow moving shape emerged from behind the doors into the light. Standing upright, his long arms hung downwards; his wrinkled face and chestnut eyes ached with sadness. The autumnal orange hair of his body was dull, dry and patchy. Despite his obvious great age his voice burned with energy and wisdom. 'I would be grateful if you would ask your dog to let the whilpet go.'

'Kirsty, put the whilpet down.' Kirsty obeyed Fiona's command and the released beast shot off up into the trees. Suddenly there was a deafening crash of thunder and large droplets of rain quickly became a downpour.

'Might I suggest that you shelter inside before continuing your journey. Please come in and take some refreshment until the rain is over.' They followed the strange old orangutan through the doors into the comparatively dry interior of the temple. Inside was vast and fairly well preserved in comparison to the outside of the building. At the far end a mildew-covered statue of a no longer worshipped god looked down upon them. Along the sides of the walls were small individual sanctuaries with iron gates, some closed, some ajar, each devoted to a distant hero or heroine. Fiona felt a sense of loneliness about the place.

'Welcome to the Temple of the Dead, my friends,' he said picking up a thick staff.

'This is where we meet the others,' Finn whispered.

The old creature led them towards the last sanctuary on the right, his staff echoing off the flagstone floor as he limped along. The large gate opened with a low creak.

'Come in please, make yourself at home.' Old tapestries and alter cloths hung on the iron railings of the sanctuary. It was comfortably furnished. A rough sandstone fireplace had been built against the wall of the temple and vented through what had once been a stained-glass window. A blazing fire and candles burning in tall silver holders added to the warmth and ambience of the improvised dwelling. A small bed sat in one corner, a desk covered with books and manuscripts occupied another. Two unrelated armchairs, one red, one green, sat either side of the fireplace.

'My name is Doblan,' he said, indicating to the others to sit. 'I am sorry the whilpets caused you bother. They can be a noisy, tiresome little tribe but they are not dangerous. They are more of a nuisance really but they will not bother you again. They are wary of me. They see me as some kind of shaman and sometimes seek my advice concerning their superstitious beliefs. In return, they bring me food and fuel for my fire. They also weave foliage over the old roof which helps keep the elements at bay.' During his introduction Doblan had filled goblets from a jug and proceeded to hand them out. 'Most of the time, however, they tend to leave me alone, which suits me well.'

Fiona and Finn pulled stools from in front of the desk and placed them between the two armchairs, thanking Doblan for their drinks. Oxterguff sat in the red armchair, nodded his appreciation and introduced everyone. Doblan leaned his staff against the wall and lowered himself into the other chair.

'Health and continued breathing,' he toasted. The goblets contained a mead which was sweet and warming and as they drank, Doblan lit a taper from the fire and proceeded to light a long-stemmed pipe. He puffed until it was well alight.

'What is this place?' asked Oxterguff.

'From what I have read,' replied Doblan, indicating the books and manuscripts on his desk, 'it was the temple of an ancient civilisation, one that ruled this land many centuries ago. As you can see, they are no more, hence its name.

'What happened to them?' asked Fiona.

'They were destroyed by a Druid sorceress named Morrigan. They never recovered and now it has been so long no one remembers anything of them except that their land was known as the world of Dracadonia. Morrigan had been banished by her own people from the upper Earth. She took over here, ruling with fear and killing all resistance. The power to rule here was passed on and fought over. Brother murdered brother, sons and daughters slaughtered parents, all for the desire to become king or queen of this disdainful realm. The present queen, Morbidea, is a direct descendant of Morrigan and is in every way just as evil. Morbidea's mother Wisteria had twin girls, Morbidea herself and the princess Morossa. It was prophesied that the oldest would grow up to become queen. Morossa who had been born two minutes before Morbidea was, therefore, destined to inherit the crown from her mother. Unexpectedly, Wisteria became very ill. No physician could discover the cause or find a cure. Even her own magic could not help her recover. She died when the princesses were only four years old. Poison was suspected but no trace could be found. The first Lord of the realm, a powerful sorcerer named Stealthman became regent. It was decided he would rule until the girls reached the age of eighteen, when Morossa would be crowned queen. In order to help fulfil the prophecy, the princesses were parted from one another. Prophecies, however, are only the predictions of wise and insightful people. It is possible there are those who wish them to be wrong. Morbidea held this wish. She had no intention of letting her sister become queen without a fight. She was determined to become the greatest sorceress ever to exist, more powerful than Morrigan herself. She studied the black arts night and day, never sleeping, gleaning black-hearted knowledge from ancient books unopened in centuries. Morossa, on the other hand, believed in the prophecy without question. She became complacent, believing that nothing could stand in the way of her accession to the throne. On the day of their eighteenth birthday a great celebration was planned. This was when Morbidea struck, destroying her sister with a spell that cast her down into the bowels of hell. Morbidea became queen and the most evil ruler Dracadonia has ever known.'

'So there is nothing left of these people at all, they all died?' asked Finn.

'All that is left are their archives, a vast library containing books and manuscripts of their history. I have spent my life studying what was written, hoping to find anything, any clue to any weakness that could help destroy Morbidea's evil regime.'

'You think the answer lies in books?' enquired Oxterguff.

'I believe answers, or at least parts of answers lie in the hearts of those who wrote the books,' puffed Doblan.

Finn wandered over to the desk. 'This is what will happen to us.' They all looked towards Finn who was holding a manuscript. 'This is all that will be left of our world if we fail. Books and bits of parchment, nothing else. They will destroy the standing stones, the cairns and wipe away all history of the Celtic people.'

'You are right, my young friend, which is why you must not fail.'

'How will we ever be able to defeat Morbidea? We are only ordinary farm children.'

'No! You are children of the blood and, as a wise sage once said, for evil to flourish...'

'All it takes is for good people to do nothing,' Fiona added, finishing Doblan's quote. 'That is what father used to say.'

'Then he was a wise man indeed. So you see my young friends, you have no choice. There is only you and those who would help you.'

'You seem to know all about us. You were expecting us, weren't you?' questioned Fiona.

'Yes, I was. That is why this place was picked as the rendezvous for your party.'

'I see, and who picked it?' enquired Fiona.

'That would have been my idea,' boomed a voice from the doorway.

'Leachim, thank goodness you are here, I am so glad you made it! Where are the others? Where's Meg?'

'They will be here soon. They took shelter in a cave when the rains began.'

'Leachim, have this seat by the fire, you're soaked through.' Oxterguff vacated his seat which Leachim happily occupied and, just as Doblan had done, he lit his pipe.

'Doblan, my old friend, it is a while since we had a pipe together.'

'An activity that I always look forward to,' said Doblan leaning forward. Leachim held out his hand and they clicked the stems of their pipes together before sitting back to puff contentedly, filling the air with smoke.

'Doblan has been a true friend to our cause. He and I met some time ago to draw up plans for your quest and his study of the ancient texts has provided valuable information.'

Doblan continued, 'What I discovered was the existence of a pendant worn by Morrigan, the first ruler of this ancient realm. It was passed down from one ruler to another and in many cases was seized or stolen when a ruler was usurped or murdered. It became regarded as the ruling symbol of power. Whoever wore the pendant had the right to rule Dracadonia. It had been passed to Morossa, as according to the prophecy, she was to become queen.' 'But she never became queen,' interjected Finn. 'Her sister killed her. Did Morbidea not take the pendant for herself?'

'No, Finn, when Morbidea unleashed her spell, literally, all hell was let loose and during the turmoil the pendant fell from Morossa's neck. When it became clear that Morossa would be destroyed and that the prophecy would never be fulfilled, her advisor Stealthman took the pendant and escaped with it. It has never been seen since.'

'Until now,' announced Leachim. Leachim, who had crossed to the fireplace, stood there with the pendant hanging round his neck glistening in the light of the fire.

Stunned into silence, every eye in the room was fixed on the pendant. It was beautiful, hanging in perfect symmetry from a strong silver chain, each link tooled to lie smoothly against its neighbour in perfect alignment. The pendant itself was circular, crafted from solid silver. Three carved raven heads connected by three golden Celtic swirls. The eye of each raven was set with a deep red ruby. Doblan was the first to break the silence.

'So I see you were successful in your mission.'

'Yes, I was, although I have to admit it was at some cost.'

'That was to be expected,' added Doblan.

Fiona moved forward to get a closer look. 'It is rather beautiful,' she said, 'but it's. . .'

'Unsettling to the eye, it has an aura of evil,' added Oxterguff.

'You are right, that's exactly it,' agreed Fiona.

'So you won't be fighting over who's getting to wear it,' quipped Finn. 'I just think it's creepy, it's like the weird birds' eyes keep looking at you. How did you get it Leachim?'

'It's a long story, you had better take a seat.' Doblin refilled all the goblets and placed a bowl of colourful fruits before the children. He and Leachim lit new pipes. When they were settled Leachim began his tale. 'After we came through the Yett, we followed the instructions of the faerie queen and split our forces. Malcolm travelled in my place as I had another task to undertake. This task involved Stealthman. After Morossa's death, Stealthman escaped into exile, taking the pendant with him. Morbidea was furious, she had become queen but did not have the pendant to consolidate her power. Many saw this as a bad omen and believed that she did not have the right to rule Dracadonia. She put a price on Stealthman's head and offered a large reward for anyone who would recover the pendant for her. Stealthman, however, had made good his escape. He had taken up residence in a bleak desert in a far-off primitive land, a land inhabited by fierce bands of warring tribesmen. Stealthman used his magic to subdue the tribes and then unite them as one. He became their leader and formed the varying tribes into a small army. For him, the failure of the prophecy had destroyed everything he held dear. He began to believe that if what was written could be unwritten, if the true queen could be usurped, then what did it matter who ruled the realm. It could be anyone, even himself, and why not, he had the pendant.'

'Stealthman plans to attack Morbidea?' Fiona's face was set like stone as she thought out the implications of Leachim's revelation.

'Yes, that is his intention. But he is not a rash or impatient man. He will wait until the time is right and victory assured.'

Fiona's mind raced as she pieced all this information together. She remembered what Leachim had said earlier, at a cost, and her thoughts flooded out. 'The pendant Leachim, how does it come to be in your possession? Stealthman gave it to you?' Leachim let her proceed, wanting to see if Fiona's powers of deduction were as strong as he hoped. He was not disappointed. 'Why would he do that? It doesn't make sense, if that is the symbol of power, he wouldn't just give it away. What was the cost?'

Leachim smiled, he felt an almost fatherly pride. 'I have entered into an alliance with Stealthman. It is dangerous but is the lesser evil. He knows of our quest. He is also aware that if Morbidea receives the powers that Meg's tail is capable of, he will never be able to defeat her. I persuaded him that if Morbidea was aware of the presence of the pendant it would distract her and give us a better chance of retrieving the tail. Morbidea wants this trinket desperately. If we can split her focus, it may give us the advantage that we need.'

'You know that you will never be able to trust Stealthman?' There was concern in Fiona's voice.

'I don't think we can trust anyone who has their mind set on gaining the throne of Dracadonia. Stealthman has already begun to employ mercenaries from other lands to expand his army and bring forward the date of his attack.'

'Just a minute,' interrupted Finn, 'Mercenaries? How many lands and realms are there in this place? I thought there was just the faerie land and Morbidea's realm.'

'The lands and their peoples here are as numerous and varied as the countries in your world, Finn, and their wars and petty differences are just as destructive.'

'How large is his army?' Fiona asked.

'It is large enough to prevent our return to the faerie realm whether we are successful or not.'

'It doesn't really get any easier for us, does it? quipped Finn. 'Why did father have to go and interrupt the witches that night. He's got no idea the trouble he's started. He should have come straight home like mum told him to.'

'You never do what I tell you to.'

'You're not mum. You're my sister. I don't have to do what you say.'

The conversation was interrupted by the sound of horses arriving outside the temple.

'That will be the others,' announced Leachim. 'I was not expecting them until after the rain.'

'I want to see Meg,' shouted Finn as he slipped through the gate and ran across the flagstones. He stopped when the doors were pushed open and a unit of heavily armed Cadaveran nuns burst in. Finn had never seen such hideous creatures. He knew at once who they were. With no time to freeze, he turned on his heels and screamed in his loudest voice, 'Cadaverans!' As he raced back to the little sanctuary he could see more Cadaverans entering from doors at the back and sides of the temple, some were abseiling down from the roof on vines, there was no escape. Finn slipped back through the gate. Doblan stood by the fire. There was no sign of Leachim or Kirsty. Oxterguff was in front of Fiona with his sword drawn.

'Finn, get behind me!' Oxterguff barked. 'Quickly.'

'No, Guffy, it's no good. There's too many of them, they'll kill you, put the sword down,' pleaded Finn.

'Do as the boy says,' nodded Doblan. 'It would be best.' The gate was pushed open and Stinkeye entered followed by her fiercest Cadaveran troops.

Chapter 22

PRISONERS OF THE CADAVERANS

Oxterguff and the children sat in chains on the floor of Doblan's chamber. Doblan remained standing by the fireplace.

'So you are the annoying little brats that have caused me so much trouble!' spat Stinkeye. Her eye had been bothering her and she was in a foul mood. Not wanting to make any more mistakes, she had decided to take charge of the operation to capture the children. 'Well, I can promise you an unpleasant journey in a very uncomfortable wagon and, believe me, I'll be keeping a good eye on you.'

'As long as it is your good one and not your stinky one,' smirked Finn, because it honks to the heavens.'

Stinkeye drew a dagger which she pointed at Finn's throat. 'If it were up to me I'd cut your tongue out right now and kill you here. The queen, however, wants the pleasure of doing that herself.'

'Exactly,' Finn agreed, 'you're not in charge. You are just one of her servants with an eye that smells like a cow's excrement.' Fiona and Oxterguff couldn't prevent letting out a laugh.

Stinkeye was furious, 'Laugh while you can, because it will not be long until you are crying, crying for mercy,' she got up and joined Doblan by the fire.

'You have done well sending your whilpets to tell us of their whereabouts. Morbidea thanks you and sends you this reward.' She handed Doblan a pouch which he opened, pouring the gold contents into his large hairy hand.

'If we get out of this I'll be back to pay you a visit, you treacherous old ape,' snarled Oxterguff.

'Spare me the heroics,' laughed Doblan. 'Stinkeye, get them out of my temple.'

Stinkeye gestured towards two burly guards and Oxterguff and the children were dragged to their feet, taken outside, and put in the back of a secure wagon. The floor of the wagon was bare and strong bars made escape impossible. A large, formidable padlock was snapped shut.

Perched high in a tree Mouldy watched as the horses were reined into action and the wagon set off.

It was, indeed, an uncomfortable journey. They were bumped and jolted as the wheels announced every stone and hole in the road. Stinkeye was not wasting any time; they didn't stop until well after dark. Fiona could not sleep. She watched the flickering firelight from the guards' campfire dance on the bars of the wagon and overheard their muffled conversation.

We should reach Raven's Neuk by early evening tomorrow in plenty of time for the ceremony,' announced one, 'I say it will be a great celebration once Queen Morbidea receives the power of the tail. I think we should drink until we are as happy as a daft donkey.'

'Me too,' said the other. 'There will be many battles ahead so we may as well enjoy ourselves.'

'You are right. The future will be fun. I have drawn up a list of all those I will wreak revenge upon. I read it every night before I go to sleep.'

Fiona turned away from the guards' conversation. She had heard a frightening reminder of what was awaiting her world if they failed in their quest.

'I can't sleep,' whispered Finn.

'Count me in on that,' added Oxterguff.

'Fiona, what happened to Leachim and Kirsty? Did they escape?' Finn asked.

'I don't know. I got such a fright when you yelled, I didn't even notice where they went.'

'They disappeared up the chimney.'

'What?' Fiona couldn't believe what Oxterguff had just said.

'Up the chimney?' gasped Finn.

'When you yelled your warning that the Cadaverans were here, he called Kirsty over and said something in that weird magic language of his then the two of them turned to smoke and disappeared up the chimney.'

'He must have a reason, he wouldn't leave us,' said Fiona. 'I just know he wouldn't.'

'That was my first thought,' agreed Oxterguff, 'but I'm beginning to wonder if he knows what he's doing. He trusted that matted old baboon, Doblan, and now we know he was a traitor who sold us down the river.'

'There's something strange about all of this. He had the pendant remember, he couldn't let the Cadaverans get their hands on that, which is probably why he had to escape and save himself,' said Fiona.

'But why did he take Kirsty with him?' said Finn.

'I don't know. There are a lot of questions needing answered. I need to think for a bit.' Fiona sat propped in a corner of the wagon and let her mind ponder on the events of the day.

Meanwhile, Mouldy reported his news to Heather and Eilean who had been sheltering, safely concealed in a cave. 'The Cadaverans were all over the place,' he informed them, 'they knew about the rendezvous.'

'How could they?' fumed Eilean. 'The faerie queen chose the place for the rendezvous, no one else could know.' A sound from the entrance of the cave alarmed them and the two girls reached for their weapons. Kirsty suddenly shot from the darkness followed by Malcolm. 'Couldn't you have called a greeting or do you just like spooking folk?'

'Sorry Eilean, got a lot on my mind at the moment.'

'You almost had an arrow through the middle of that mind,' joked Heather. 'I take it you know the children and Guffy have been captured.'

'I was there, or rather Leachim was. Doblan, the old ape, betrayed us. He sent his whilpets to fetch the Cadaverans. I escaped with the pendant. I couldn't let it be captured.'

'Why did you bring Kirsty with you? Would she not have been better to accompany the others? She could have been useful to them,' added Heather.

'Cadaverans hate dogs. Many of them were savaged or gnawed at by dogs when they were hanged. They would have killed Kirsty.'

Kirsty gave a small whimper and sidled up between the two girls.

'Don't worry, Kirsty, we'll get any Cadaverans that even look in your direction,' soothed Eilean. Heather gave Kirsty a reassuring scratch behind the ear.

'We need to move,' said Malcolm taking charge of the situation. 'Eilean, you take Heather and Mouldy with you. I want you to track the children. The Cadaverans will be taking them to Morbidea. You must stick close and find out exactly where in the city they take them. This will be vital if we are to help them escape.'

'What about you?'

'I will travel with Meg and Kirsty to Raven's Neuk by a separate route. I will not be far from you but I need to make contact with an accomplice I have in Dunraven. I have an important job for her.

In the wagon, Finn was getting restless. Fiona was sitting with her knees up to her chest, her arms folded across them and her chin resting on top. Her eyes were fixed ahead seeing nothing in particular. Finn knew she could sit like this for ever, letting her thoughts roam goodness knows where. How she could sit quiet for so long was something that he could not understand. He was however, quite the expert at bringing Fiona out of her reverie.

'Fiona, do you think Stinkeye's ever had a sweetheart?' Oxterguff guffawed and Fiona let her forehead fall onto her arms and giggled with laughter. 'I think she has,' he continued. 'Probably someone with their nose missing.' The others snorted into their sleeves. 'Imagine if they ever got married. 'Do you No-nose, take Stinkeye to be your awful-wedded wife?' Oxterguff's hearty chuckle encouraged Fiona's laughter even more.

'Oh, Finn, stop it. You're making my sides hurt and I can't believe what you said to her today about her eye smelling like a cow's. . . you know what.'

'What did I say?'

'Don't! You're not going to make me say it, it's a horrible word. I don't know where you heard it from.'

'I learned it in school.'

'No, I don't believe that for one minute.'

'It's true! Do you remember that big book of words that the teacher brought in?'

'It's called a dictionary.'

'That's it, I saw the word in there.'

'Mr Campbell never let anyone touch it. He just gave us out words that he wanted us to learn.'

'Remember he used to keep a bunch of us in after to clean the classroom? Well, we all used to clean up as quickly as we could and then me, Gary Cairns, Colin Cornwall and Spike would get the book and look up rude words. Do you want to hear some?'

'No, I don't. You really are a disgusting child. Now go to sleep.'

'My favourite is a long word, beginning with F...'

'Stop it,' laughed Fiona.'

'And ends with E.'

'I don't know what that is and I don't want to know, now go to sleep.'

They settled down but some seconds later a voice in the darkness broke the silence. 'Flatulence!' whispered Finn, 'it means fart.' For the final time that night they giggled amongst themselves until they fell asleep, Finn smiling with satisfaction.

Chapter 23

THE ECCENTRIC ALCHEMIST

The following morning the children woke early. The dampness had seeped into their bones and they were very cold. Oxterguff snored in his corner of the wagon. As the sun rose in a grey sky the Cadaverans broke camp and prepared to continue the journey north to Morbidea's castle. The prisoners were given a crude breakfast of stale bread with a bowl of milk to dip it in.

It wasn't long before the wagon was rattling on, jerking and bumping the inmates about. The children held tight to the bars to give themselves some stability. The guards were chatting relentlessly about the forthcoming ceremony. What the prisoners and guards did not know was that the chatter and noise was making it very easy for Eilean and Heather to shadow their journey.

Meanwhile, Malcolm and his four-legged friends were making excellent progress. They were two hours ahead of the prison wagon and hoped to stretch that lead by another two and arrive at the city gates in the afternoon. Malcolm was sure that would be enough time for the next part of his plan. They halted briefly at a small stream for Meg and Kirsty to drink and for Malcolm to fill his water skin.

'We're fairly shifting,' commented Meg. 'I take it you have an appointment with the contact you mentioned. Do you have a spy in the city?'

'Not so much a spy as a concerned individual. I need her to carry out some experimental work for me.'

'Will it help us in our quest?'

'It could, depending on how things work out.'

'Who is this individual?'

'Her name is Sharagon. Some would say she is a simple alchemist. I would say she's an absolute genius.'

'Can she be trusted?'

'Yes, I believe so.'

'If I might remind you, you... and Leachim... you trusted Doblan and he betrayed us.'

Malcolm took hold of Meg's bridle and looked her straight in the eye. 'Only because I asked him to betray us,' he said solemnly. 'It was my plan to have the children captured.' Meg could not believe what Malcolm had said, 'What? What did you say?'

'You heard me. I have had to make some difficult decisions but none more so than arranging for the children to be captured.'

'Why, why have you done this?' Meg whinnied.

'Morbidea had the forest surrounded. They would have been caught and possibly killed trying to escape. This way we know where they are, where they are going and when they will get there.'

'We know where they are going alright,' said Meg angrily. 'Straight into Morbidea's clutches. She will kill them, knowing they are children of the blood. What have you done?'

'Listen to me, Meg. I didn't make this decision easily. We are facing an enemy of great power. We have to be cunning and take chances we would not otherwise have taken. Morbidea will not kill the children right away. She will want them to see that they have failed, to see the extent of her power before she destroys their bloodline for ever.

'She won't kill them right away! That's fine.' Meg's voice was laced with sarcasm.

'It gives us time, Meg. Besides, they have Guffy with them. Eilean and Heather are trailing them too, they will not let them out of their sight. We will find a way to rescue them.'

'You had better be right, because if anything happens to these children. . .' Meg's voice trailed off, it was a prospect she did not want to consider.

'I do understand, Meg, but we have to believe and have hope.' They left the little stream and galloped on as their thoughts raced ahead of them.

By mid-afternoon, Morbidea's capital lay before them. Towering on a hill high over the city was Raven's Neuk and on the slopes below a vast urban landscape sprawled in its shadow. A drab expanse of dwellings, taverns and work buildings stood tightly packed together. To the right were the docks, where a dingy cluster of warehouses hugged the coastline. Smoke from a thousand fires formed a layer of smog that hung over the city like a brown blanket. The castle rose through this dense lowering murk drawing the eye toward a dark and turbulent sky.

'Welcome to Dunraven,' said Malcolm without smiling.

'Wouldn't be my first choice for a home,' added Meg. 'What do you think, Kirsty?' Kirsty lay down and put her paws over her eyes and made a gruff throaty sound which made Malcolm smile.

'Let's go.' The three comrades headed towards the city and soon reached the main gate. There were troops in the streets and Malcolm was pleased to note that they were all soldiers of the regular army, no Cadaverans were anywhere to be seen. As Malcolm approached the gate the guard on duty stood to attention and saluted him as he passed through. As they made their way they were absorbed in the hustle and bustle of the city; there was an air of excitement as the inhabitants prepared for the royal ceremony. Food and drink seemed in plentiful supply as laden carts were carried and hauled through the narrow streets.

Malcolm dismounted in front of two huge wooden doors. The one on the left had a smaller door inset into it. Malcolm knocked. Behind a grill a viewing panel slid open. He leaned forward to speak. The small door opened and Malcolm stepped through closing it behind him. Seconds later the larger door opened slowly allowing Meg and Kirsty to enter. Meg noticed the tallest and thinnest servant she had ever seen. He was easily two foot taller than her head height.

'Thank you, Link. Is your mistress in the lab?'

'Indeed she is sir, never anywhere else these days.'

Across the cobbled courtyard a set of wooden stairs climbed up to a balcony which ran the entire length of the building. Below the balcony were three arches; one that gave access to a stable and the others to living accommodation at ground level. Malcolm crossed to the foot of the stairs and called up.

'Sharagon, it's me, Malcolm. Are you busy?' He turned to Meg. 'She doesn't like to be disturbed if she's in the middle of an experiment. Sharagon, are you there?'

A loud explosion blew the door at the top of the stairs wide open and a blackened net curtain danced briefly before disappearing over the rooftop. Smoke began billowing out of the door followed by a youngish woman who emerged coughing through the smoke. She leaned over the bannister.

'Malcolm, it's you. How lovely to see you,' she spluttered. 'Don't worry, that was exactly what was supposed to happen. How's my hair, is it on fire?'

'I don't think so,' replied Malcolm.

'Even better then, do come up. Tell Meg to go into the furthest away stall in the stable, I'll bring her up on the service elevator.' Sharagon disappeared back into the room waving away the smoke away as she did so.

'She's on our side?' asked Meg quizzically. 'And what's a service elevator?'

'You'll soon find out. Last stall on the right.' Meg trotted into the stable as Malcolm and Kirsty climbed the stairs. When they entered Sharagon's laboratory, the tall servant was operating the rope of a large bamboo fan venting the smoke up through a skylight in the roof.

'I'm working on this fascinating stuff, Malcolm. It's a bit volatile but when I can find a way to stabilise it there's no end to what it could be used for. Science is definitely the way forward, Malcolm, magic has had its day.'

'I don't know if Leachim would agree with you on that,' said Malcolm with a smile. Sharagon pulled on a long metal lever releasing a mechanism that caused the floor of Meg's stall to move upwards and soon she was with the others in the laboratory.

'What is that stuff?' asked Malcolm with genuine interest.

'At the moment I call it bangy stuff because, well, that's what it does. It's made from three different substances which in themselves are harmless but when mixed together are wonderfully bangy. The bang you just heard was only three little spatulas full. Can you imagine what a barrel load would do?'

'I'm imagining what a small jar might do. How does it bang?'

'Either with a naked flame, or hit it with a force, or drop it, sneeze on it, blow too hard on it and in one case talk too loud near it. It has already killed a Cadaveran.'

'Really? How did that happen?' asked Malcolm.

Sharagon looked sheepish. 'Oh! Just accidentally really. She had a toothache. I thought I could use the bangy stuff, just a pinhead of each mind you, to blow the sore tooth out, but it blew all her teeth out.'

'Ouch,' said Meg

'And her head blew off as well. But the toothache went away so we're always learning. What can I do for you Malcolm?'

'Well, as you know, Morbidea's ceremony takes place tonight.'

'Goodness! So soon, I get so caught up in my work I lose track of time.'

'We need to stop her and I wondered if you could do something for us with this.' Malcolm took the pendant from under his tunic and handed it to Sharagon.

'You have been busy. If Morbidea gets this as well as the power from the grey mare's tail, there will be double evil to deal with. No force of magic or possible science would be able to overcome her power.'

'That is why she must never get her hands on this, but perhaps if we had another just like it. Do you think you could make a copy from gyre metal, if you have any that is?'

Sharagon, looking coy, fidgeted with a loose thread on her worn grey lab coat. 'What makes you think I would ever be able to get my hands on gyre metal. There's none left in the entire realm.'

'Sharagon, if I may pay you a compliment, you are the worst liar I have ever met.'

'No really, Morbidea ordered every alchemist in the realm to destroy all existing stocks. She says its magnetic properties interfere with her magic.'

'So, you are telling me you destroyed all your gyre metal stock because she commanded it?'

There was the tiniest pause before Sharagon replied, 'Yes, all of it. I didn't even keep any of it bubbling in the volatile safe.' Sharagon was rearranging spatulas and stirrers in the top pocket of her lab coat, her darting eyes avoiding contact with Malcolm.

'Alright, I believe you,' said Malcolm giving in.

'You do?' replied Sharagon in a surprised tone.

'Of course I do. You wouldn't be able to keep more than forty cubits bubbling in the volatile safe anyway, would you?'

Sharagon suddenly became very excited and animated, 'That's where you're wrong, Malcolm. I've devised a way to keep one hundred and eighty cubits bubbling in there. It was quite simple really. All you have to do is. . .'

'Yes, carry on my friend. You were saying one hundred and eighty cubits, is that correct?'

'You tricked me Malcolm, that's not fair.'

'No, I just know you well. You are too dedicated and brilliant to destroy anything that would hinder your experiments.' Sharagon seemed happily embarrassed and her pale elongated face blushed red.

'I reckon you could make a rough copy of the pendant in a couple of hours.'

'Humble puff! I'll have a perfect copy in twenty minutes. I have been working on something quite special.'

'Remember, the gyre metal has to resemble gold and silver.'

Sharagon stared at him. 'Any more obvious information you would like to give me? Right, let's get started.' She took the pendant over to a work bench and carefully removed the chain. Next she made an impression of both in a bed of sand and clay. Putting the chain back on the pendant she hung it in a silver cabinet with a sealed glass door. Meg, Kirsty and Malcolm watched intently. Using a set of long tongs she took a jug of molten gyre metal from the volatile safe and poured the shiny thick fluid into the mould. Within five minutes it was set. When she tapped it out of the mould it looked terrible. The chain was rigid and although the metal was the correct shape it was still the colour of the original gyre metal.

'I take it that is not the finished article?' asked Meg. Sharagon gave her a withering look through her lab goggles as she bent the chain into a circle and fed it through the eye of the replica pendant.

'It will not be the finished article, as you call it, until we do our sub-molecular vibratory transportation,' she boasted as she placed the replica into a second silver cabinet directly opposite on the other side of the room. She carefully weighed and measured a number of chemicals from thick glass-stoppered bottles labelled 'Astringent of Mars', 'Saffron' and 'Oil of Vitriol' then she placed the mixture in a small bowl and put it in the cabinet with the replica pendant. Adding a final pinch of 'Philosopher's Wool' she quickly closed the door.

'Right! Here we go.' Within seconds the chemicals spontaneously combusted, the cabinet began vibrating and a strong humming sound emanated from both it and the cabinet across the room

'What happens now?' asked Malcolm.

'We wait. Let me explain it simply for you. The original pendant is in what I call a transportation chamber and the replica with the gyre metal is in the reception chamber. The particles of both pendants telepathically link and the gyre metal atoms take on the properties of the original pendant's atoms and we get what looks and feels like a perfect copy.

'That is it in simple terms, is it? You never cease to amaze me,' smiled Malcolm.

'It's a new theory I'm working on, I call it my Quacktum Physics.'

'Sounds well-named if you ask me,' put in Meg. 'Let's hope it works.'

'If you don't mind, mare,' said Sharagon somewhat hurt, 'I'd rather not have negative equine thoughts in my lab during experiments,' and at that she pulled the lever and Meg disappeared back down to the stables.

Malcolm chuckled, 'She doesn't mean to be negative, she's a horse with a lot on her mind.'

The sound of humming from the cabinets began to die down and Sharagon turned her attention to the one holding the replica. Opening the glass door she excitedly extracted the pendant. It was in every aspect identical to the original. Malcolm marvelled at the beauty of it.

'Shar, you are a genius. No one would ever be able to tell the difference,' he said giving her an appreciative pat on the back.

'Most people wouldn't, but you plan on giving this to Morbidea.

Such a thing will likely have an effect on her sorcery. It might not take her long to discover the pendant is the cause. If this happens, let's just say it could be the end of the tale.'

'It is a chance I will have to take. It may buy us some time. Can you keep the original pendant here, somewhere safe?'

'Of course I will. You know you are my favourite earthling.'

'And you are my favourite eccentric alchemist or is it scientist?'

'Science can make a big difference, Malcolm.'

'I believe it can, which brings me to my next question.' Malcolm leaned forward and whispered in Sharagon's ear. She looked at him, concern in her eyes and smiled.

'Very well, you are determined to get yourself into trouble, aren't you?'

Sometime later the trio crossed the cobbled yard and through the large doors finding themselves back in the street. Malcolm instructed Kirsty to go back to the main gate. She was to stay there and wait for the wagon with the children to arrive then join with Heather and Eilean.

'Meg and I will head up to the castle and wait for you along the road. We will then begin the most dangerous part of our quest.'

Chapter 24

RAVENS NEUK

Kirsty lay inconspicuously beneath an old trestle table, her eyes intent on the main gate of the city. It was a good spot: she could clearly see all who were entering. Her nose twitched and her eyes flicked every time there was a movement at the gate. Suddenly her nose caught a recognisable scent. She sniffed deeply. There was no doubt it was Oxterguff. This was followed by the familiar scents of Finn and Fiona. Kirsty waited patiently. Her ears picked up the sound of wagon wheels and soon the prison wagon was in sight. Upon reaching the gate the driver reigned in her horses and spoke to the guard on duty.

'Prisoners for the queen.'

'Take them straight up to the castle. They are to be put into the cells in the Weeping Tower,' instructed the guard.

The wagon jerked on its way and the prisoners got their first glimpse of Raven's Neuk. It was a massive inhospitable structure. Towers and ramparts outlined the top of the castle. A series of bridges and walkways criss-crossed the façade connecting the many fortified areas. A sinister-looking tower was attached to the corner of the castle right on the cliff edge. The tower itself rose two hundred feet above the castle walls while the drop to the sea below was a terrifying thousand feet. At intervals, rising up the tower and jutting out from the stonework, were what looked like three large bells. Adjacent to each bell was a small wooden door set into the tower.

'Guffy, why are there so many bells on that tower?' asked Fiona.

'They're not bells Fiona,' explained Oxterguff, 'they're cages. Morbidea likes to put her best prisoners in those cages. She can watch them hang there in all weathers like unloved pets until they die of starvation and cold.'

Eilean and Heather had kept as close to the wagon as they dared without arousing suspicion. As they passed the guard they overheard the mention of the Weeping Tower. Kirsty caught up with them making her presence known with a sharp bark.

'Excellent,' cried Eilean. 'Are Malcolm and Meg here too?' Another bark confirmed this. 'Good, let's get after that wagon and free Guffy and the bairns before they get to the tower.' They spurred their horses into a gallop with Kirsty sprinting ahead.

'We can take them,' shouted Heather as they gained on the wagon. 'We'll have the element of surprise attacking from the rear.' She knotted her reigns and began controlling the horse with her knees as she slid an arrow into her bow. Eilean drew her sword from her scabbard. It was at this point they noticed a heavily-armed detachment of Cadaverans galloping out of the main castle gates. They had been sent to escort the wagon safely inside. All they could do was reign in their horses and break off their attack. Slightly further on, they halted and watched as the wagon was escorted into the castle and lost from their sight.

'By the clan's teeth, that was close,' fumed Eilean, 'we almost had them.'

'We were lucky. If we had engaged they would have been upon us like flies. We'll have to see if we can find an entrance into the tower from inside the castle.' They watched as Mouldy's silhouette soared towards the Weeping Tower. They still had their eye in the sky. Inside the castle the three prisoners were dragged from the wagon and escorted down a long corridor. They were ushered through a small side door where they entered into a vast hall. Fiona and Finn knew exactly where they were. Dappled light flooded into the hall through stained-glass windows. Magnificent wooden horses were carved to form the supporting beams of the roof, their hooves dancing out into the roof space. Ornate double doors announced a grand entrance at one end of the hall, large enough for three coaches to enter side by side.

'This is the place,' gasped Finn. 'This is the Grand Hall. This is where it all began!'

'And this is where it will all end.' The strong voice startled them. It echoed throughout the hall, eerie and with the resonance of evil. 'Bring the brats to me now,' it commanded.

The guards escorting the prisoners pushed them towards the elevated black marble dais at the end of the hall. In the middle, Morbidea sat on an imposing silver throne. Its high back was carved with three silver ravens, the one above her head with wings outspread. Two silver serpents with gaping fanged mouths formed the armrests. Standing by Morbidea's right was Stinkeye, displaying a hideous smug expression.

Morbidea leaned forward, 'So you are the children of the blood, come to retrieve your precious tail, am I right?' The children stood saying nothing. 'They're very rude, Stinkeye. Do you think they would answer my question if I killed their little faerie friend?'

'Stop! I will answer your question,' replied Fiona in her most courageous and defiant tone. 'Yes, we are the children of the blood and we have come for the tail.'

'Very good, girl. Seeing as you are so good at answering questions, I'll ask you another. Who else is with you on this foolish quest and do not insult me by lying?'

'Don't tell her anything, Fiona, I'd rather die here for my queen than give her any more information,' snapped Oxterguff passionately.

'That is easily arranged. Guard!'

As the Cadaveran guard drew her sword Fiona leapt forwards. 'No! Leave him, I'll tell you.'

'Stop, Fiona,' interrupted Finn. 'Don't tell her anything.' Pointing at Oxterguff he added, 'He's just our guide, let her kill him, we don't need him anymore.' Oxterguff was astounded at Finn's outburst and shot him a look of disbelief which Morbidea was quick to register.

'Does the faerie guide live or die?' barked Morbidea, 'It's up to you girl, but I want an answer. I am in no mood to be toyed with.'

'Leachim Widdershin is leading us. He is the one who planned the entire quest.' Morbidea sat back in her throne her hands on the silver serpent heads, her long slender fingers stroking the fangs. She looked pleased with the result of her interrogation.

'He hasn't done a very good job has he? Who else travels with him?'

'He travels with our horse and our dog and for some reason an owl. We separated in order to avoid detection. He came through Antler Pass and we travelled over the top of the mountain,' Fiona was thinking on her feet. She knew that Paul, Morbidea's spy, had probably told her everything about the makeup of the group so she reckoned she was not giving away anything that Morbidea didn't already know. She did not want to reveal the existence of the underground lake.

'And where is this wizard now?'

'We don't know, when your Cadaverans attacked us he disappeared. We haven't seen him since.'

'He sounds like a bit of a cowardly wizard really.'

'No, he's not,' shouted Finn. 'He's a great wizard. He turned me into a cat and got my own dog to chase me.' Morbidea's laughter resounded around the great hall and, as if following orders, Stinkeye and some of the guards joined in.

'You poor fools, that is the sort of trick I learned when I was three-years old. This second-rate magician has duped you to embark on a quest that is now going to end in failure and your death. Take them to the tower.'

Oxterguff jumped forward, 'Give me a sword!' he demanded. 'I will fight as many of your Cadaverans as you like. I will die here fighting with a sword in my hand.'

Morbidea's anger erupted, she stood from her throne pointing at Oxterguff. 'You will die as I decide, like an animal hanging in a cage, swinging from the walls of my tower. You will die weeping for your mother! Now get them out of here. Take that faerie guide to his cell.' Calming slightly, she added, 'The brother and sister can be imprisoned together. It will be nice for the sad little siblings to spend some last time together.' As the guards began escorting them from the hall Morbidea spoke again. 'One moment, it is only fair that I share with you your fate. Tonight during my ceremony a demon will be summoned, one who has been waiting for thousands of years. He will be conjured at the height of the ceremony and follow my commands; my first request will be that he devour you both. Tonight your blood will curdle in the veins of the demon and your threat will die forever.'

Finn was suddenly so terrified he burst out, 'Tonight, tonight, tonight, is that all you can think about?' Finn's heart was racing. 'What about tomorrow? Have you thought about what you're going to give it for its breakfast? And someone who isn't me is going to have to take it for walks? You really shouldn't get pet demons unless you've thought about what it takes to look after them.'

Morbidea eyes grew wide causing a sea of wrinkles across her forehead. No one had ever answered her back.

'We'll see if you feel like joking tonight. Take them to the cells,' she hissed. Morbidea sat back on her throne seething, watching the departing group when Finn's voice rang out once more.

'And Demon is a terrible name, what about Fluffykins, that's a nice name?'

The door closed leaving only Morbidea and Stinkeye in the Grand Hall. 'Get your Cadaverans to keep a watch for this Leachim character and the beasts that are with him and tell them to be careful. He knew enough of our ways to kill four of your best. He could still be a threat.'

'Very good, Majesty,' Stinkeye bowed and retreated from the hall leaving her queen in pensive mood. Morbidea sat her fingers indented by the serpents' fangs. There really was something about those children that irked her. She would be relieved to see them devoured and dead.

Chapter 25

THE SECRET TUNNEL

Heather and Eilean had reunited with Malcolm and headed towards the castle of Raven's Neuk.

'We need to find the secret tunnel,' Leachim said its opening is hidden among the rocks near the cliffs.' He produced a strip of black silk material from his tunic. 'This is from Stealthman's cloak, the one he wore when he made his escape from the castle. In his haste his cloak snagged on the rocks leavings shreds of it behind. That is where Kirsty comes in.'

'Surely after all this time the scent will have gone cold,' Heather offered.

'I hope not. Come on, Kirsty, do your work girl,' Malcolm knelt down and held the strip of cloth under Kirsty's nose. She sniffed intently and gave a small snort, then with her nose in the air she set off along the base of the castle wall. Back and forth she went stopping here and there to investigate further. She covered the same area three times without success. Suddenly a swift breeze rolled up from the sea over the cliff edge. Kirsty's nostrils sniffed the air. She trotted towards the edge of the cliff, her moist nose twitching. Crawling on her belly she moved right up to the very edge and waited. The rest of the group crawled up beside her and peered over the cliff edge.

'Down there!' Eilean pointed to a set of old worn steps which led down to a hole in the cliffs.

'Well done, girl,' said Malcolm giving the collie an appreciative pat on the head. 'Meg, you and Kirsty wait here with the other horses. We need you to be ready for a quick getaway.'

'Just you make sure you find the children,' said Meg. 'Good luck.'

Malcolm and the girls lowered themselves over the cliff and made their way down the broken narrow steps to the entrance of the cave. Beyond the entrance lay a tunnel which was high enough to stand upright in. Walking a little further in, they came across a crate containing several wooden torches. They were old but dry and luckily when Malcolm struck a flint they lit easily. They set off along the passageway and, as they ventured further in, the floor began to rise in a gentle upwards slope.

'What part of the castle does the tunnel take us to?' whispered Eilean.

'I believe it's somewhere near to the Grand Hall. I'm not exactly sure.' A short while later the tunnel came to an end at what appeared to be a wooden doorway. There was no sign of a handle. An old makeshift ladder lay by the wall alongside it. Two tiny dots of light, eye-width apart could be seen about eight feet up. Eilean leaned the ladder against the wooden panel and Malcolm climbed up to look.

At the top of the ladder he noticed there was a brass indentation in the shape of a face, the two holes through which the light seeped were the eyes. He put his face into the indent and although not a perfect fit, he was able to see to the other side.

'I can see lots of wooden panels,' he informed them. 'There are brass plaques above each one, like the one I'm looking through now. There must be a way to open this. See if you can find some kind of mechanism.' Eilean and Malcolm began hunting for some kind of releasing mechanism when Heather gave a little double cough. She was holding a rope which was attached to the side of the panel.

'If you have a secret tunnel, I guess you don't have to hide the opening mechanism,' she smiled pulling on the rope. The panel began to move. It was noisy and stuck a couple of times but eventually it opened enough for them to get through.

'I hope no one heard us,' murmured Eilean.

Malcolm put his head out. They were halfway down a long corridor. He noted a studded doorway at one end but there was no sign of life. 'It's clear!'

'Wait a minute! You go out,' said Heather, 'I'll close it from the inside. You see if you can work out how it opens from out there.' Malcolm obediently stepped into the corridor. Heather pulled the rope. From the other side Malcolm observed a slight movement in the brass plaque as the panel slipped back into the closed position. Stepping forward, he reached up and pressed the base of the plaque. The panel re-opened effortlessly and silently. The girls stepped through. Malcolm closed the panel.

'It's easy when you know how,' he smirked. 'Let's try to get our bearings. What about that studded door?' suggested Malcolm moving swiftly towards it. The door had a sliding viewing panel behind a rectangular grill. 'There could be a guard,' cautioned Heather. The sound of the bolt being pulled back had them jump to the side. The door opened outwards and, luckily, they were hidden from view behind it. Suddenly, a dozen little whilpets came whizzing through the door and down the corridor. They were dressed in smart white shirts. A Cadaveran guard stepped from the other side of the door to shout after them. Eilean's hand went to her sword.

'You were supposed to be here ten minutes ago, you useless monkeys. This place has already been security checked. You're lucky I'm letting you through.' The guard turned and pulled the door closed behind her, muttering about what she'd like to do to the hairy little creatures. The door was bolted angrily. Malcolm and the others let out a silent sigh of relief. Heather was about to step forward when the sliding panel was slid open. She crouched and pressed herself against the door, just inches below the viewing grill.

'I eat monkeys, you know!' The panel slid closed and the others held their breath a moment longer.

'That was close,' Eilean whispered.

'Too close. I could smell her breath,' grimaced Heather. 'And she probably does eat monkeys.'

'It appears we are in a secure area,' Malcolm said quietly. 'If all the entrances are guarded it may be difficult for us to get into the main hall. I think we should backtrack to see if we can find another way.'

Chapter 26

THE WEEPING TOWER

The prisoners were brought to the guard room inside the tower. Oxterguff was put into a small solitary cell and the children in the one next to him, the only separation being solid iron bars running from floor to ceiling. The children were somewhat relieved that they could at least see and speak to Oxterguff. The guard locked the cells and hung the keys on a rack at the other side of the room. She closed the solid wooden door behind her and the sound of bars and bolts banged solidly on the other side. They were taking no chances. There were no windows in the cells, light came from a candle on a table which sat below the key rack and from torches burning on either side of the door. A small doorway was set in the wall to the far right of the guardroom.

'Not quite the outcome to the quest I had imagined,' grumped Oxterguff, 'especially for someone who is only a guide, one that isn't needed anymore.'

'I'm sorry, Guffy, I really didn't mean it. Fiona told me to say it.'

'He's right, Guffy, it was only to protect you and to throw Morbidea off the scent. I'll explain everything later but right now we need to find a way out of here.'

'Not much chance of that,' bemoaned Finn. 'We can't reach the key and even if we did that door is solid and bolted on the other side. What about that other little door? I wonder where that door leads to.'

'There's only one way to find out,' said Oxterguff standing and stretching. 'We'll get the keys and have a look.'

'And how do you plan on doing that?' asked Finn.

'I just happen to be an expendable guide with something up my sleeve.' Oxterguff put his arm through the bars, turned his palm toward the ceiling and from below his sleeve Purdy crawled out.

'Purdy! I thought we lost him when the guards took your satchel. Are we glad to see you, Purdy?' Finn gave the puddock a stroke on the head.

'He was too quick for them. He jumped up my sleeve before they took my satchel. So, Purdy, we need those keys hanging on the wall over there.' Oxterguff placed Purdy on the floor where he checked out his task. One leap onto a stool and a second onto the table had him just three feet below the keys. Working out his angle he shifted and shuffled until he got into the right position. Pausing for a second, Purdy launched himself like a shot from a canon. A quick sound of metal on stone and there he was, hanging from the iron key ring. Purdy wrestled the ring off the rack and dropped to the floor with the keys, making a clanging noise as he landed.

'That was brilliant, Purdy,' laughed Finn with a glint of hope in his eye. 'You're a genius.'

The puddock's tongue shot out and wrapped around the keys as he backed towards Oxterguff's cell, dragging his prize with him. In no time Oxterguff had the door to his cell open and was freeing the children.

'I don't care if he is a puddock,' smiled Fiona, 'I'm giving him a kiss,' which she did. Purdy puffed himself up into a heroic pose.

'Watch out, Fiona,' said Finn. 'If he turns into a handsome prince you'll have to marry him.'

The initial joy of escaping from their cells subsided as they turned their minds to the fact that they were still locked in the guardroom. They listened carefully, straining to hear any sounds beyond.

'I don't think there is anyone out there. I'll try the door.' Oxterguff gave the door a hard push, then he pulled, but there was absolutely no movement at all. 'There is no way that is shifting.'

Finn went over to the smaller door. 'This one has a bolt on the inside, it must lead somewhere.' He slid back the bolt, pulled the door open and all three recoiled in horror. Silhouetted against the evening sky, swinging a thousand feet above the sea was a skeleton slumped inside a bell-shaped metal cage. Its bony fingers gripped the cage and its skull peered through the bars in a desperate deathly gaze. They stood in shocked silence. Suddenly the skeleton spoke.

'I wondered when you'd open the door.' All three jumped back shrieking in unison.

It wasn't the skeleton. There, clinging to the side of the cage was Mouldy. He swooped from the cage through the open door and landed on the table where he warmed himself by the candle. 'Do you always keep your guests waiting outside?'

'Mouldy! It's so good to see you. Are the others here?' Oxterguff was keen to figure out what their chances were.

'First things first,' tooted the owl. 'I'm starving. Have you got any food?'

'Sorry, Mouldy, we haven't got a thing, we're all hungry,' Finn answered.

'What about that puddock?' Purdy leapt up Oxterguff's sleeve and kept going until he was well lodged under his armpit.

'You are not getting to eat Purdy. He's our hero,' Finn informed him.

'Very well. In answer to your question, Oxterguff, yes everyone is here. Meg is waiting with the other horses to make a swift getaway, if we ever do get away. The others found Stealthman's escape tunnel and used it to get into the castle but I have no idea where they are.'

Oxterguff's mind was working hard. 'That's some good news at least.'

'Do you think they'll be able to find us in here?' Fiona asked the owl.

'I know they will give it all they've got but, for all we know, they could be the ones in need of our help.'

'You're right,' agreed Fiona. 'Somehow we have to get out of here ourselves.'

'There is only one way we can do it.' Finn was standing close by the door, the cage and its bony occupant hanging eerily behind him.

'Finn, come away from that door, it's dangerous.'

'Staying in here is dangerous!' replied Finn with his head poking out from the doorway, looking upwards.

'Finn, did you hear me? I said come away from that door. What are you looking at?'

'I'm looking at the walls of the tower to see if there are any hand or footholds on the stone.'

'Are you mad? You can't possibly think you'd be able to climb out there. You'd be killed for sure. One slip and you would be gone for good.' Fiona's voice was fretful.

'I know, and tonight when I'm being devoured by that demon I'll definitely be gone for good and so will you. If I had a choice I'd rather fall a thousand feet.' Fiona felt numb when she realised that Finn was serious. It wasn't just an idea, he was actually planning on trying to climb the tower.

'No! I won't let you. I absolutely forbid it.'

'Fiona, you are the best big sister I could ever have but you have to see there is no other way. We are trapped here and somebody has to try something. No one else can climb like me. I'm the lightest, my feet and hands are the smallest. I can get into crevasses that no one else could. This is the only way out.'

'Guffy, tell him this is insane. Tell him he'll kill himself.' Oxterguff looked at Fiona, his eyes steely.

'I can't Fiona. The boy is right. I will not ask him to do it. We can wait for them to come or take our chance this way. Finn is the only one amongst us equipped to try it.' Fiona was stunned into silence. She looked back and forth between the two of them, thoughts numb in her head. She sat down on the stool. Finn came over and knelt beside her, leaning on her lap.

'We're in a terrible place, Fiona, and it's not fair. We might only be children but it's up to us. We can't give up now. You have been so brave. All I've done is get caught by fish and made a nuisance of myself. Leachim would not have let me come if he didn't think I could be of some help. Maybe this is my chance? I'm a really good climber. Remember that time I climbed the crags near the Stoogrie Burn?'

Fiona didn't look up but spoke tenderly. 'You fell off. Remember? I had to come and get you.'

'I made it to the top. I only fell on the way back down.' Fiona smiled. 'Anyway,' Finn added, 'I'm better at climbing up than down and that's the way I'll be going.'

'I don't like it, Finn, I really don't.'

'Well, one of us that is me has to do it this time!' Fiona laughed loving Finn's nonsense way with words. 'Anyway, Mouldy will be able to guide me. He can hover and tell me where to put my hands.'

Fiona closed her eyes and took a deep breath. 'You better be careful, don't you dare take any chances.'

'I won't, I promise.' Fiona grabbed him and hugged him as tight as she could. Finn hugged her back then tried to break free. 'Let me go now,' he whispered. 'Guffy's looking.' He sat on the floor and took his shoes off. 'I can climb better in my bare feet,' he announced. Guffy came over and gave Finn a strong handshake. 'Good luck, lad.'

'Thanks, Guffy,' Finn had the strangest feeling in his stomach. He wasn't sure if he was nervous or excited but Oxterguff's handshake made him feel brave. Everyone was dependent on him succeeding. That had never happened in his life ever before.

Mouldy suggested that he should maybe start by trying to reach the metal bar that the bell cage hung from. He flew back out onto the cage as Finn moved into the doorway. A blood-red moon hung overhead, illuminating the waves that crashed onto the black rocks far, far below.

'Nice night for a paddle,' he quipped.

'Stop joking and concentrate,' snapped Fiona angrily.

'Sorry.' Gripping the wooden upright of the door frame with his left hand he carefully turned and holding as tight as he could, his right hand and foot began feeling along the outside of the tower for any foot or hand holds.

'Try and keep three points of contact at all times,' chipped in Mouldy. The fingers of Finn's right hand quickly found a ridge in one of the stones which gave a good grip and was long enough, if need be, for him to hold onto with both hands. His toes felt furiously for a foothold, finding one about a foot out from the doorway. With his fingers latched onto the ridge of the stone and his foot firmly on the first hold, he pulled himself out from the warm glow of the doorway. Quickly, his other hand clamped the ridge of the stone and he clung there, his left foot suspended in mid-air. He suddenly became aware of the wind as it blew around the tower. Bringing his left foot up beside his right he did a little jump putting his left foot where his right had been, giving Fiona a massive fright.

'Don't do that, Finn, you're meant to climb it, not dance on it.'

'I needed my right foot free to find the next toehold,' Finn called back. 'Besides it's not as hard as it looks. A lot of the mortar has come loose so there are spaces to hold onto.'

'Didn't you listen to what Mouldy said? Three points of contact at all times. Don't you dare do that again!'

'Alright, I promise.' Finn climbed carefully up towards the iron bar. Swinging his leg over it he was able to perch there and rest for a moment. Looking down at Fiona and Oxterguff he could see their concerned faces peering up at him. Far below the waves smashed upon the rocks. Above him he could make out another door with its torture cage hanging opposite. This door was closed too and he guessed he would have to climb all the way to the top. Bracing himself against the wind and the cold he resumed his climb.

Finn worked himself up so that he was standing on the iron bar and took a second to work out the best holds. 'It's not easy but not as hard as I thought it would be,' he said to himself. Mouldy appeared, hovering beside him. 'None of the other doors are open, Finn, you'll have to climb all the way to the top.'

'I thought I might,' he puffed pulling himself further up the tower. A wide gap in the stonework higher up became visible, offering a really good hold and he reached up for it with a huge effort and gripped it with his entire hand. After a couple of breaths, as he pulled himself hard towards it, the entire stone came away and Finn fell back losing all contact with the wall of the tower. He was falling. Somewhere he heard Fiona scream.

'NO!'

He stretched towards the wall but there was no way he could ever make it. In his fall Finn had spun over and could see the rocks below. It's still better than being devoured, was the thought that whizzed through his head, when bang! He hit something that knocked the wind from him. Finn instinctively grabbed and then stopped. He had caught onto the cage and was swinging crazily, one hand holding the bars, his feet and arm waving about in mid-air opposite the doorway where Fiona and Oxterguff stood with stricken faces. The skeleton was dislodged and its arm fell through the bar wrapping around Finn's shoulder. He screamed, pushing it away. The arm snapped off and spun a thousand feet to the sea below. Finn watched in panic as it spiralled down. Fiona and Oxterguff held their breath as Finn pulled himself onto the cage and, shaking terribly, climbed back up to the iron bar. He was back where he started.

'Could you try not to do that again,' asked Mouldy who had landed on the top of the cage beside Finn.

'I'll do my best not to.' His knees and feet were bleeding and his hands were scratched. 'At least I'm not hurting.'

'That's probably the adrenalin pumping through you,' Mouldy informed him.

'I don't know what that means but I hope it's a good thing.'

'I would get moving again before it wears off.' Once again, focussing hard and testing the strength of every hold, Finn started to climb. He passed three doors with cages and was becoming aware of the aches and pains from his injuries when the top of the tower came into view. Immediately his spirits rose. He didn't know how much longer he would have been able to go on but seeing the battlements at the top of the Weeping Tower gave him a renewed energy. With the last of his strength he reached the top and with superhuman effort he pulled himself over the parapet where he lay panting on the ground. Mouldy landed beside him.

'Well done, Finn. That was incredible. We need to keep going. Let's see if we can find a way back to the others.' Finn got to his feet. In the middle of the tower was an inner wall capped with a conical roof. He circled round the wall in a clockwise direction looking for some kind of entrance. Halfway round he found a door. Finn lifted the latch. The door opened.

'That was lucky,' whispered Finn.

'See if you can get down to the guardroom. I'll go and tell the others that you made it.' Mouldy flew back over the parapet to give the others the good news. Finn quietly made his way down the narrow stairs, the smooth cold stone felt good and solid beneath his feet. There was no one else about. It looked as though the tower was empty apart from the lower floor where they were being kept prisoner. Reaching the door to the guardroom he lifted the heavy wooden bar; sliding the bolts at the top and bottom he pulled the door fully open.

Fiona's arms were wrapped around him before he could even step inside.

'That was the worst time of my life, don't ever do that to me again.'

Oxterguff clapped him on the back. 'Well done, lad. That was quite a feat. You showed what you're really made of.' Finn carefully put on his shoes and jacket. He felt elated and ready for anything.

'Right' proclaimed Guffy. 'Time to go and see if we can find a way to spoil Morbidea's party?

Chapter 27

PLAN OF ATTACK

Aware that time was against them, Eilean, Heather and Malcolm were feeling frustrated. They had tried several doors all of which were locked and they were effectively trapped in the corridor.

'There has to be a route from here to the main hall,' suggested Heather. 'In order for Stealthman to get into the tunnel we just used, he would have had to escape from the hall into this corridor.'

'You're right,' said Eilean. 'One of these other panels must lead to the hall.'

'It has to be the one directly opposite,' reasoned Heather. 'I mean, if you're in a hurry to escape you want the shortest route. Malcolm immediately pressed the brass plaque on the panel directly opposite the one they had come through and, to their relief, it slid open. He stood aside letting his friends through, giving Heather a well-done slap on the shoulder as she went by. They pulled the rope inside and the panel closed.

They found themselves inside a dark wooden framework. As they moved further in, the headspace got lower causing them to crouch down. They could hear the mumbling and grumbling sound of activity. Above the din orders were being shouted and questions called out. Rays of soft light were shining in through three grills further away in the darkness. They made their way towards the source of the light. Peering through the grills they stared in disbelief.

'Wow! We've done it,' whispered Eilean. 'We're under the dais in the great hall.' Goosebumps tingled down her arms.

'This is where the ceremony will take place,' Malcolm whispered back, hardly able to conceal his excitement. They could see the large entrance doors at the far end of the hall. Black marble pillars and enormous stained-glass windows towered above. Running down either side were lavishly laid dining tables upon which silver shone and glass sparkled. A mass of servants rushed about arranging and rearranging. Large candelabra that had been lowered to the floor were now lit and being pulled aloft, laden with a thousand new candles, their ropes straining as they were tied firmly in place.

A commanding voice echoed through the Great Hall. 'Enough! All is ready. Leave now.' The servants scurried off and silence descended.

The three friends crouched down, listening intently.

'At last, Stinkeye, the time has come.'

'Yes, Majesty.'

Malcolm's eyes widened and surprise animated the faces of the two girls. Queen Morbidea was standing directly above them, separated only by a slab of marble. They hardly dared to breathe. Morbidea's footsteps echoed as she made her way down the steps of the dais, Stinkeye following by her side. They stopped on the bottom step. Malcolm and the girls stared wide-eyed through the grill. The queen and her Cadaveran commander stood a few feet away with their backs to them.

'Summon the demon, Majesty,' pleaded Stinkeye excitedly, 'one last time before he appears for ever to do your bidding.' Morbidea crossed the floor to a large circle which was tiled with signs and symbols understood only by the queen herself. Raising her hands her sordid voice called out.

What was written I have erased,
Now time for my plan of Earth's decline,
By the cursed blood of the ancients,
The power of the tail will be mine.

A hideous, high-pitched sound emanated from below Morbidea's feet, accompanied by vibrations and rumblings. The hidden friends looked on as the circle on the floor began to disintegrate. The signs and symbols revolved in the air around Morbidea, bright as stars, orbiting the queen like planets – an evil solar system, herself the dark sun in the centre. The floor beneath her had vanished and from glowing embers and dancing flames came the cries of a demon, fierce and wailing.

'Patience, my precious, it is not long now, soon you will be free to serve me. Tonight I have a delicious request, I would like you to devour the children of the blood.' The roar that came from the unseen beast was terrifying causing the three friends to grab hold of one another. Morbidea lowered her arms, her spell subsided and once again she stood on the floor of the great hall.

'All is ready, Majesty. Tonight the power concealed in the grey mare's tail will finally be given to you,' said Stinkeye.

'Indeed and with the children of the blood gone forever we will be able to bring destruction and death to their land. I will destroy the memory of my Celtic ancestors forever. My armies will flood through the Yett and the Earth will be added to the realms of Morbidea for all eternity.'

'You will be the greatest most powerful queen the world has ever known. My Cadaverans will have their revenge and spread a fear never before known among the Earth dwellers.'

'Now we must go and prepare ourselves. Seal the hall. Let none enter until I command.'

The concealed friends waited a while before daring to speak.

'What was that hideous creature?' asked Eilean. 'Did any of you see it?'

'No, hearing it was enough for me,' replied Malcolm. 'We have to find Fiona and Finn. Let's get out of here. As they begun to crawl away from the light Eilean felt a sharp tug on her hair. Feeling with her fingers she untangled a lock which had caught in a bit of rough splintered wood. Eilean looked up.

'Wait, I think I might have found something.' A square perimeter of light shone faintly above her head. 'Look at this.' She pushed the square outline. It was heavy but moved slightly. 'It's a trapdoor.' She and Malcolm pushed until it folded back on itself. One by one they pulled themselves through it. They found themselves directly behind Morbidea's silver throne, the marble trapdoor leaning on the back of the throne itself.

'We need to find an area that could give us a vantage point,' Eilean informed them.

'What then?' Heather enquired. 'We don't have a plan and we don't know what happens during the ceremony.'

'One thing we do know,' added Malcolm, 'is that at some point it includes the wee beastie that lives down there.' They all glanced at the circle of symbols on the floor. 'We at least know we have that to deal with.'

'I'd like to think we could get the tail and be out of here before she summons that thing.'

'I agree with you Eilean, but we can't bank on that happening. We know she's got the children and we're shut in here unable to help them. We need to get the tail and stop her summoning the beast and sacrificing the children.' They spent some time exploring the hall before meeting back, secure in the shadows of the marble pillars.

'Suppose all goes well and we get the tail and free the children,' said Eilean, her voice quiet but firm. 'The scenario is that six of us along with the tail will have to get through the trapdoor, escape through the tunnel, scale the cliffs and make our getaway on the horses. The probability is we will be seen and they will come after us. It doesn't bode well for our chances does it?'

'I agree, so I have a plan,' Malcolm informed them. 'It is literally a long shot. Heather, how many arrows do you have?'

'Not enough to take on all the Cadaverans that will be about.'

'Well, whatever you do, make sure that you keep two in reserve because we are going to need them.' An unexpected sound came from the shadows. Within seconds swords were drawn and Heather was poised with her bow ready to shoot.

'Watch that door,' hissed Malcolm. They waited, Heather moving behind a statue where she had a clear shot through the legs of some marbled hero. All attention was fixed on the door as the handle squeaked and the door slowly eased open. Three small figures emerged from the other side.

'Guffy! Late as usual, I thought we were going to have to do this on our own.' Guffy's hand had automatically reached for a sword that he did not have when he realised it was Malcolm's voice he was hearing. Fiona and Finn were ecstatic to see Malcolm. They were introduced to Eilean and Heather. Brief summaries of respective journeys were exchanged, the highlight being Finn's remarkable feat which he shrugged off pretending it was nothing at all. Inside however, he was glowing with pride.

'I can't believe we have all made it here,' said Fiona. 'Do you think it is possible that we just might succeed?'

'We're not out of the woods yet,' Eilean informed them. 'Technically speaking, all we have managed to do is get ourselves locked in this place until our enemies arrive and we become vastly outnumbered. We do, however, have the element of surprise which we have to use to our best advantage. Meanwhile, I think we should inspect every aspect of this hall and make a note of anything that could be advantageous to us.'

'Good thinking, Eilean,' agreed Malcolm. 'Heather, could you and Guffy start by trying to remove that grill beneath the dais? I have an idea.'

As they set about their task, Heather handed Oxterguff the sword she had been wearing. 'You might as well have it. I prefer the bow.' Heather and Guffy found that the grill could be removed quite easily. They tried a couple of times and then put it loosely back in place so as not to arouse any suspicions.

Finn and Fiona found a white marble statue of two hunters restraining a pack of hounds. Finn thought it would be a good spot to hide as it gave them good cover and a great view down the length of the hall. Fixed to the wall next to it was a rope anchoring one of the huge candelabras that hung from the ceiling. Finn thought that if the rope was to be cut or undone the candelabra could be dropped from its great height causing mayhem on the enemy below.

Heather and Guffy returned to Malcolm and Eilean with the good news about the grill and all four put their heads together in a council of war. Soon everyone was briefed on the plan and their part in it. There was nothing left to do but to go to their respective hiding places. Heather settled herself under the dais near the grill, her quiver of arrows resting nearby. Fiona and Finn got themselves comfortable among the straining hounds and Eilean, Malcolm and Guffy found themselves places among the shadows. All they could do now was wait.

Chapter 28

THE CEREMONY

Time passed slowly for the six waiting warriors. No one had entered or arrived and Finn was beginning to get bored.

'I'm hungry, all my scrapes hurt and so does my mouth where the hook went in.'

'You've certainly been in the wars,' Fiona agreed. 'I was thinking, do you think if we get out of this alive we'll ever be able to go back and live our normal lives on the farm?'

'Three meals a day and a warm bed with no demons wanting to devour you. Yeah! I certainly can. I miss Mum,' Finn sighed.

'Me too.' Fiona knew, however, that life would never be the same again.

It was not long before activity began in the hall. Servants appeared and the sound of guests arriving outside had risen to a great clamour. Cadaveran guards arrived taking up their positions. Several guests commented that it should be the general's troops in charge not these hideous creatures. The hall was soon full and Malcolm began to mingle amongst the guests. Eilean and Oxterguff stayed in the shadows. The orchestra struck up, playing music which boasted great victories of the past, arousing patriotic stirrings among the loyal subjects of the queen. Some stood to attention with tears in their eyes, others joined in. Then the conductor began Queen's Morbidea's anthem. There was a huge cheer, trumpets sounded and a squadron of Cadaverans made their way through the majestic double doors of the hall. There must have been a hundred of them and in the middle, borne on an elevated chair, was Morbidea herself. She wore a gown of fine grey silk and from her shoulders hung a white cloak embroidered with silver thread. Her raven black hair was set with a glistening silver tiara. The cheering was deafening as she was carried down the length of the hall. Reaching the dais she was lowered to the floor. She stood and ascended the marble steps. Following behind was Stinkeye and Seneca, the army's soothsayer. Reaching the throne she turned to her subjects, Stinkeye on her right and Seneca to her left. She raised her hands and within seconds the hall was silent. Morbidea sat on her throne. Seneca addressed the assembly.

'Welcome, everyone, to this historic ceremony where a long-awaited almighty power will be imbued upon our illustrious Queen Morbidea. With the tail as her talisman she will march into the land of the Earth dwellers, destroying them forever and adding their world to our realm. Bring forth the tail. Let the ceremony begin!'

A sudden clap of thunder produced a look of shock on Morbidea's face. This was not part of the ceremony. This had not been rehearsed. A flash of lightning caused the great doors to burst open and down the length of the hall galloped General MacMorna, his horse Scathach reared to a halt in front of the throne. Dismounting, he knelt in front of his queen.

'Majesty, I have news of an invasion. Lord Stealthman, your sister's traitorous advisor, has raised an army. He has crossed the border to the south west and marches here to our capital.' The news caused an upheaval in the hall, everyone speculating as to what would happen and what to do.

'Then why are you here?' barked Morbidea. 'Go forth and intercept him!'

'I have only one battalion which is already on its way to confront him. His numbers are superior. The rest of the army is deployed to the south for the attack on the Earth.'

'Go general. Do what you can for now. When the ceremony is over I will join you and crush him forever. Go now.' The general bowed, swung onto his horse and galloped off up the hall. 'Bring forth the tail. Let the ceremony begin.' There was now a hint of panic in Morbidea's tone and low-level murmuring among the guests continued. Trumpets blew as a troupe of Cadaverans entered the hall. Floating between them in mid-air was the tail. It was exactly as Leachim had described, a beautiful silver-tooled handle with the hairs of Meg's tail billowing from it. When the Cadaverans reached the foot of the dais Morbidea stood raising her hands causing the tail to soar above her until it hovered directly above her silver throne.

'Bring the children of the blood to me now.' Guards marched off to fetch the prisoners as Morbidea strode onto the floor in front of her symbolic circle. 'I summon Raminal from the realm of the deep. Come to me, my loyal servant.' The symbols pulsated with light and Morbidea's evil universe orbited around her once more. The sound of the demon could be heard as fire flamed from the depths into the hall. Morbidea's subjects watched in fear and awe.

The children watched but their eyes were fixed on the tail, so close but so far from their grasp. Suddenly Fiona knew what they had to do.

'Finn! The rope, we need to untie it. Not this one, the one holding the candelabra near the dais.' Finn and Fiona scrambled down from their hiding place, dodging between the guests, until they reached the pillar where the rope was tied off. They tried to untie it but it would not budge. Finn sighed. Oxterguff arrived by their side. Grabbing the rope he pulled with all his strength and managed to get enough slack for the children to undo the knot. 'Let it go, Guffy,' yelled Fiona. Oxterguff let the rope go and the candelabra plummeted towards the ground. As it did so the rope began to shoot skyward up through its pulley. 'Grab it, Finn, grab it!' The two children grabbed the rope, hanging on as tight as they could as they were pulled at speed from the floor of the hall up towards the rafters.

Heather had removed the grill and witnessed the children being pulled towards the roof space. Swiftly she placed an arrow in her bow. Malcolm was poised with a glass jar of Sharagon's bangy stuff. The agreed plan was for Malcolm to throw the jar into the mayhem of the spell being conjured above the demon. Heather would then put an arrow through the jar causing a massive explosion. He moved close and was about to throw when the chandelier hit the floor with a tremendous crash. Realising what was happening he held tight to the jar trying to judge the right moment. He couldn't risk the children being injured by the blast. The weight of Finn and Fiona hanging on the rope caused it to behave like a large pendulum. They were swung back high into the rafters gripping on with all the strength their fingers could muster. Far below them the fierce glow from the demon pit shone upwards spreading tongues of fire, casting an orange sheen onto the tail.

'Here we go!' shouted Fiona. The rope swung them low and fast, speeding downwards towards the pit of the demon before carrying them aloft once more. Malcolm knew his timing would be crucial and readied himself. He watched intently as the children swung over the pit soaring past the outstretched arms of Morbidea. Then he launched the jar. It sailed in a perfect arc descending into the middle of the circle. On cue, Heather released her arrow, it shattered the glass and, as the explosion rocked the hall, Fiona and Finn let go the rope, grabbed the tail in mid-air and were blown behind the throne. The blast flung Morbidea backwards, her ceremonial outfit singed and smoking. Her ears were ringing and there was utter confusion amongst most of her Cadaverans. One, however, had witnessed Malcolm throw the jar and was on him in seconds, sword drawn. Eilean and Oxterguff saw the attack and were now engaged in a fight for their lives as more Cadaverans joined the fray. Swords flashed and clanged as steel parried steel. Oxterguff took a slash to the shoulder but fought on like a cornered tiger. The three comrades formed a circle, back-to-back, in order to give each other some protection but they knew they could not last long as they were becoming vastly outnumbered.

Heather was still in position below the dais, desperately waiting for the smoke to clear. She couldn't see her second target but knew the safety of her friends depended on her hitting it as soon after the first explosion as possible. A noise behind startled her. It was Fiona and Finn. After landing they had dropped unobserved through the trapdoor. They were now safely below the dais with the tail firmly gripped in Fiona's hand.

'You got it! Well done, well done.' Heather quickly checked and although the smoke was dispersing she still could not see her target. 'Quickly, this way.' Leading the children to the secret panel she opened it for them, crossed the corridor and opened the second one. 'Pull the rope on the other side to close it and make your way to the end of the secret tunnel. Steps will take you up to where Meg and Kirsty are waiting.'

'What about Guffy and the others?' pleaded Finn. 'I won't go without them.'

'We'll join you as soon as possible. Please go, there is no time to argue.'

Heather turned, heading back to her hiding place. Back in position the smoke had cleared in patches. She could just make out the slight glint of the large glass jar which Malcolm had placed in a nook beside the great doors at the far end of the hall. She had only used one of her arrows and, despite having a full quiver, she knew she needed to get it with her first shot. Slipping the arrow onto her bow she pulled back until it was fully taught and took aim. Just before she let fly something caught her eye to her left. Eilean had slipped and a Cadaveran with raised sword was about to strike. Swiftly she readjusted her shot and the arrow pierced the throat of the attacker, the blade falling clear of Eilean. Heather's next arrow was in the bow before Eilean had jumped to her feet. A second of concentration and she released the bow string. It was a long straight shot that flew down the entire length of the hall. It felt like an eternity before it reached the target but when it did the resultant explosion was magnificent. The massive doors were blown apart. The stained-glass windows erupted, causing rainbow hailstones to pour down on the fleeing guests. Two of the main beams in the roof buckled and hung dangerously above. The terrified subjects panicked and screamed. Even the Cadaverans began to run for cover. None of them had ever seen such destruction. Noise deafened them and smoke filled their corrupted lungs. Every creature present looked stunned as they took in the level of devastation. Even Morbidea staggered, looking around dazed and reeling, trying to make sense of what had happened.

In the midst of the confusion, Eilean, Oxterguff and Malcolm had made their way to the trapdoor. This diversion had been part of the plan to enable them to get to the escape tunnel undetected. Malcolm helped Oxterguff through the trapdoor and Eilean followed closing it behind her.

'Did they get the tail?' was the first and only question on her mind.

'Yes, they got it,' answered Heather with a huge smile on her face. There was a moment of utter exultation as they grabbed and shook one another.

'I suggest we get out of here fast,' grinned Eilean. 'Are you alright,

Guffy?'

'I will be, lead the way.' They were soon making their way along the escape tunnel in pursuit of the children. Everything had gone to plan but they knew the wrath of Morbidea would not be far behind them.

Chapter 29

MORBIDEAS FURY

Morbidea stomped through the debris of the Great Hall towards her throne, anger fierce and raging within her. Humiliation seeped from every pore. She had been made to look weak. Her realm was under attack, her armies dispersed throughout her lands but more than anything the tail was gone, the one thing that could give her unlimited power. It must be found at all costs.

Seneca and Stinkeye stood at the foot of the dais, Stinkeye bleeding from a gash above her good eye. Seneca's hair and clothing were singed. They were both too terrified to speak. Morbidea sat bent on her throne. Her voice shook.

'The children of the blood have escaped. They have taken the tail. Why has this happened? Tell me why I have not received what is rightly mine?' Her voice was low, almost quivering, creating terror in the two figures cowering before her. 'Seneca! Why did you not foresee this? Your job is to warn me of such things. You have failed me.' Seneca's eyes were wide, fear coursed over her skin.

'Majesty, I... I...'

'FAILED ME!' Morbidea's hand shot out towards Seneca's throat and, although she stood some distance from her, Seneca felt a lethal grip around her neck. She couldn't breathe. Morbidea raised her off the ground to the rafters where she hung choking and gasping, pleading helplessly as she kicked and struggled. Morbidea's left hand pointed at the circle on the floor and once again the fire from the pit erupted. The demon below could be heard wailing in anger at not being released as promised. 'You will explain your failure to the demon.' At that she brought her arm down with a fury that cast Seneca into the fiery pit. She waited a short time for all to hear Seneca's cries and with a wave of her hand the circle was once more in place. 'Find them, Stinkeye. I want the tail back and those brats caught. They cannot be far. You know your fate if you fail me. Now find them!'

Stinkeye immediately began issuing orders and putting a search party together. It was then she noticed one of her dead Cadaverans with an arrow through the neck. Kneeling for a closer inspection she noted the arrow had gone in at the base of the neck and was pointing at an upward angle. She looked back in the direction the arrow must have come from and there on the steps of the dais was a rectangular hole. In their hurry to get away Heather had not put the grill back in place.

'Look, Majesty, this arrow was fired from under the dais.' Within seconds the Cadaverans were crawling all over it.

'Commander, there is a trail of blood here, leading behind the throne. Within moments they had found the trapdoor. They followed Oxterguff's trail of blood showing them exactly which panel accessed the escape tunnel. Seconds later Stinkeye was leading her troops down the tunnel in pursuit of their enemy. Morbidea followed. She would take no chances now and was annoyed that she had not killed them when she had the chance.

Further along the tunnel Heather suddenly stopped and gestured to the others to be silent. They stood listening and heard muffled sounds in the distance.

'They have found the entrance. I thought it would have taken them longer. I reckon they are only minutes behind us.' No one spoke. They moved on quickly and soon reached the mouth of the cave. Climbing the steps swiftly they found Finn and Fiona already mounted up.

'They're not far behind us,' Eilean informed them as she and Heather swung up onto their horses.

'Get going now!' Malcolm ordered. 'Head for Sharagon's. She's expecting you.'

'What about you?' Eilean demanded.

'I have one final surprise for Morbidea. Now go, I'll meet you at Sharagon's shortly.' The horses were spurred into action and the fugitives were soon galloping off to be lost in the warren of the city.

Malcolm returned to the top of the cliff. Crouching beside a rock he had a good view of the steps from the cave. Reaching into his tunic he pulled out his last small jar of bangy stuff. He didn't have long to wait before the Cadaverans reached the mouth of the cave. Stinkeye ordered them up the steps and as they charged Malcolm stood and launched the jar. The explosion blew the steps apart, sending the Cadaverans plummeting from the cliff side. Morbidea and Stinkeye had no choice but to turn back. Malcolm mounted his horse and galloped off towards the city.

Morbidea and Stinkeye raced back along the tunnel. Morbidea ordered, 'They can't get far. Get to the cliffs and find their tracks. Seal the city. I want every house, every shed, every cupboard searched and deploy the dracoscope. Anyone aiding them will be fed to my demon. They are trapped in my realm and they will not escape. Go now!'

Chapter 30

THE FORTUNES OF THE WONDROUS FINOLA

Arriving at Sharagon's, the fugitives were admitted by her tall servant Link. Sharagon appeared briefly from her laboratory onto the balcony.

'Go into the house, I will join you shortly.' She disappeared back into her strange and wondrous domain. Another equally lanky servant, identical to Link, approached and they began to turn two iron handles causing a large tarpaulin to be pulled across the courtyard. Link noted that Finn was watching them closely.

'Camouflage, young man,' explained Link. 'It is to stop Morbidea's dracoscope from seeing what we do. This way folks.' They followed Link's long gait across to Sharagon's living quarters. It was apparent she had been expecting them. A large fire burned and there was enough seating for all as well as a space to accommodate Meg. There was an assortment of food laid out and the ravenous band ate heartily and eagerly recounted their adventure. Fiona informed the others of the reason Leachim had betrayed them and how his gamble had paid off.

'So Doblan didn't betray us,' mused Oxterguff, 'I feel bad about calling him a flea-ridden old ape now.'

'Excuse me,' Fiona asked one of the Links, 'do you think Sharagon has forgotten we're here?'

'I'll go and get her,' announced Finn jumping from his chair. 'I want to tell her how brilliant the bangy stuff was.' A short time later Finn returned with Sharagon who received much praise for her wonderful invention.

'Now that you have refreshed yourselves,' she added, 'we must implement your escape. Morbidea has sealed the city. Her guards are checking every wagon and cart so you must listen carefully to what Leachim has planned for you. Come with me.' Sharagon led them to the stables, in the middle of which stood a large wagon. It looked well-used and was painted in fading colours of red, green, blue and gold. On the sides of the wagon painted in an arch of large letters were the words 'The Wondrous Finola'. Beneath the arch were painted the words 'Fortune Teller', 'Star Gazer' and 'Soothsayer'. Signs and symbols of the zodiac were depicted at various points on the wagon. Finn felt there was something quite spooky about it.

'We must work quickly. Morbidea's troops are rounding up all the children in the city in the search for Finn and Fiona. Leachim's plan is that Eilean will drive the cart and Heather will play the part of the Wondrous Finola. Your faerie gifts will help you convince anyone who is too inquisitive. There is a secret compartment in the floor of the wagon. Fiona, Finn and Guffy will have to conceal themselves in it. It will be very cramped but, hopefully, you will only have to hide in there until you are clear of the city. Eilean, you will travel as Finola's servant. Mouldy and Kirsty will obviously be able to make their own way out of the city and follow the wagon until you stop. Meg, I'm afraid you look far too good as a commander's horse. We are going to have to dress you down.' At this point the two Links entered with a tub of mud and a collection of faded ribbons and gaudy rosettes. One began to smear the mud over Meg's black coat while the other began to plait the ribbons into Meg's mane and tail. Finn joined in helping with the plaiting of the ribbons in Meg's tail. By the time they were finished and she was yoked to the wagon she looked a sorry sight. Just what you might imagine a well-travelled workhorse would look like.

'You girls must get rid of your guard uniforms, put on these old clothes.'

'That's a pity,' Eilean sighed, 'I've grown quite fond of mine.'

'Me too,' added Heather.

'Needs must.' The two girls exchanged a quick glance and snapped to attention.

'Yes, Sir!' they echoed in unison.

'Very funny,' smiled Sharagon. Once changed, Sharagon explained the inside of the wagon to them. It contained two sleeping cots, cooking pots and utensils. There was also a shelf displaying charts and documents relating to stars and planets, with an array of crystals, straw doll figures and magic totems hanging from hooks.

The children were first up to squeeze into the secret compartment. Oxterguff was next. He lay down in the middle with his head between Finn and Fiona's feet. They had to lie on their backs with their heads turned sideways and by the time Heather's bow and quiver were fitted in, along with Eilean and Guffy's swords as well as the tail, there was only just room enough to breathe. The false floor was fitted over them and all the wagon's belongings were replaced covering the hidden compartment.

Eilean climbed up into the driver's seat and took the reins, Heather, as her mistress Finola, sat on the bench beside her.

'Good luck,' smiled Sharagon. 'I hope we meet again.' The girls nodded and Meg started to pull her precious cargo out across the covered yard. The Links opened the large double doors and the wagon exited out onto the street turning towards the main gates of the city. Mouldy immediately took to the sky as Kirsty scampered off on her own. It wasn't long before she was back under the trestle table opposite the main gate. She wanted to make sure that the wagon got clear of the city and she intended to be ready to distract the guards if a distraction was needed.

The city itself was in turmoil. Soldiers were searching houses and rounding up children who were taken away to the castle to have their identities checked. There was an atmosphere of complete upheaval. Citizens were losing their tempers as soldiers ransacked their properties.

The wagon bumped along. Inside the hidden compartment it was dark, cramped and very hot.

'I hope we will not have to be in here for too long,' whispered Fiona. Oxterguff was not enjoying it at all. He was used to living and even sleeping in the open. If they were caught there wasn't even room to put up a fight.

'Guffy, can you promise me something?' asked Finn quietly.

'If I can, I will. What is it?'

'Promise me you won't do a flatulence in here.' All three began to giggle and snort with laughter. It was agony laughing in such a tight space.

Heather and Eilean exchanged unbelieving glances as the laughter sounded from behind them. Eilean shouted into the back of the wagon.

'Will you three shut up. You'll get us caught. Be quiet.' The others realising the seriousness of their predicament, stopped immediately.

Meg was trying hard to play the part of a worn-out horse. She dropped her shoulders and haunches and made her back sag. Arriving at the main gate she let her head and neck drop even further making her look like a pathetic old nag. Soldiers were busy checking anyone that was leaving the city. Eventually it was their turn. Three soldiers motioned them forward and then signalled for them to stop. Kirsty watched quivering from below her trestle table.

'Well, well!' exclaimed the guard. 'What have we got here, a fortune teller? I could do with a bit of good luck, couldn't I lads?' he joked with the other two guards. 'Can you tell me what the future holds for me?'

Heather held her hand out. 'You must cross my palm with silver, then I, the Wondrous Finola, will tell you all that I see in the stars.'

The soldiers laughed heartily, 'And where would a poor sergeant like me find silver to waste on a cheating, lying fraud like you?' Heather looked deep in the sergeant's eyes and as she did her pupils dilated. Her eyes changed colour from green to red, a gift possessed by some of her species in the faerie realm.

The blood drained from the sergeant's face and he drew a deep breath. 'I see that you will soon have plenty silver, sergeant. You and your friends here will win lots of silver in a great battle.' The soldiers smiled, their faces lighting up with greed. Then Heather added, 'You will die rich men.' The smiles on the soldier's faces fell away as the news sank in. The sergeant looked quite shaken.

'You mean we will die soon after? Can't you stop this happening?'

'Me, but I am just a cheating, lying fortune teller.'

'No! No, you're not. I didn't mean it, please, it was a joke. You are a great fortune teller. Anyone can see that. Please help us.'

'Very well!' exclaimed Heather. 'Once you have searched my wagon I will tell you how you can avoid your fate.'

The soldiers hurriedly checked the wagon. The sight of the charts and straw dolls unnerved them and they conducted their search very quickly. They were desperate to know what had to be done to cheat fate and prevent their premature deaths.

'All good,' confirmed the sergeant. 'Tell us what we have to do.'

Heather gave them a small pouch containing a quantity of herbs and instructed them to grind the contents into hot wine on the stroke of midnight. Once the wine was drunk they would be safe and her prediction would not come to pass. As she finished her instructions her eyes resumed their normal green hue. The superstitious soldiers seemed relieved and thanked her profusely before letting them go on their way, even insisting that she take a small silver coin for her trouble.

Eilean drove the wagon through the main gate turning south in the direction of Stealthman's forces. It wasn't long before Kirsty and Mouldy caught up with them. At a safe distance from the city, they pulled into a clearing, emptied the wagon of its contents and helped the others from their stifling hiding place.

Breathing the cool air soon had them feeling better. Finn moved his arms and neck to ease the stiffness and bent to stretch his back when a wee 'thwack' hit him on the backside.

'Ouch!' He turned to find Fiona with a stick in her hand. 'What was that for?'

'For being a disgusting little grub and making us laugh when we were cooped up in there.'

'It was a joke.'

'I thought it was funny,' laughed Oxterguff.

'I know, it was quite funny,' admitted Fiona. 'Come here,' She gave Finn a big hug before joining Eilean and Heather.

'How come she can hit me with a stick and then give me a cuddle?'

'Because she's your big sister and she loves you,' answered Oxterguff.

'I don't mind the cuddle, it's the stick that my bum's still remembering.' Oxterguff put his arm round Finn's shoulder and guided him to join the others.

'That was a clever trick, Heather, you certainly got those guards worked up. I must admit though, I did not like sitting there with no sword to defend myself,' said Eilean as she strapped her sword back on over her raggedy dress.

'I'm just glad to have my bow back within easy reach,' agreed Heather as she stashed it behind her seat on the wagon. 'Do you want to know something else? That potion I gave the guards was a laxative.' There was general laughter throughout the group. Mouldy's head chuckled up and down and Kirsty gave a yappy bark.

'That's brilliant, Heather,' laughed Finn. 'That means they'll be. . .'

'I think we know what that means, Finn,' interrupted Fiona sharply. 'We don't need you to elaborate.'

'Where's the pendant?' asked Heather.

'Here it is,' Finn handed it to her and she put it over her head, dropping it inside the neck of her dress in order to conceal it.

'And the tail? We don't want that to fall into Stealthman's possession.'

'I left it in the secret compartment of the wagon. I thought that would be the safest place for it,' explained Finn.

'Good thinking! Now we should get on our way again. The sooner we find Stealthman and give him the pendant, the sooner he'll march against Morbidea and we can begin the journey home.'

Eilean and Heather climbed onto the wagon. Fiona, Finn and Oxterguff decided to walk alongside being glad of the exercise.

Walking beside Meg, Finn chatted to her about the events of the last few days. Kirsty was happy to run along beside them as Mouldy did a circuit of aerial spying before settling on the wagon beside the girls. They travelled for the whole day finally stopping to set up camp. They all helped to prepare a hearty meal which they enjoyed around a campfire.

The following day around mid-morning Mouldy returned from one of his missions to report that a group of Stealthman's mercenaries were not far ahead. A short time later they came upon them as they emerged from trees and surrounded the wagon. They were a fearsome-looking lot, wearing long loose robes that hung to their ankles. Some had large swords tucked into belts. The blades of the swords were curved and widened out sloping to a point, like large meat cleavers. On their heads they wore turbans, the end of which hung down round their necks and shoulders like a scarf. Finn remembered seeing drawings in a book at school of people dressed like them.

Their leader stepped forward. 'Where are you headed, if I may ask?' His stern features broke into a broad smile which seemed to completely transform his character from fierce warrior to benevolent traveller.

'We seek the camp of Lord Stealthman,' Heather informed him. 'He is expecting us.'

'Indeed he is, which is why he has sent me to escort you to him. My name is Omar. We are glad you got here safely. If you will follow us we should reach him in a couple of hours.' Finn took an instant liking to this man and as they set off he decided to get to know more about him.

Omar's troops seemed to take a curious interest in Oxterguff. They had never met anyone like him before and they were intrigued that someone so small could be a warrior. They asked many questions as the band travelled along.

'I've seen drawings of people like you in my world. They live in a desert,' Finn informed Omar.

'Then they are sensible people,' laughed Omar, 'I have no time for these forests. There is no open space and you bump into things all the time. Give me a wide beautiful desert any day.'

As predicted, they entered Stealthman's camp a few hours later. There was a large stockade covering an area of about two square miles. Campaign tents stood around the edge and in the centre was the marquee where Stealthman himself resided.

'Remember what Leachim told us,' Fiona whispered, 'he is a great and powerful wizard. We must keep our wits about us and get out of here with the tail as soon as we can.'

Omar dismissed his troops and disappeared into the marquee. He soon returned to tell them that Stealthman would see them shortly. He departed informing the guests that it had been a pleasure to make their acquaintance and that he hoped they would meet again.

It was not long before Stealthman arrived. There was no great explosion of smoke and light, no great effort to impress them with his powers. He simply lifted the flap of the tent and strode towards them. He was dressed similarly to Omar in a long robe of black satin with the sash gathered at the waist. No dagger or sword hung from his waist. He was a tall and stern-looking man. He eyed the group with serious interest.

'So you are Widdershin's band of adventurers. He seems to have chosen wisely. You don't look much but I believe you managed to steal the tail away from Morbidea. Allow me to offer my congratulations. Do you have my pendant?'

Heather stepped forward and lifted the chain over her head, placing it into his outstretched hand. Studying the pendant carefully he paused and looked at the others. There was a brief look of suspicion, then his face broke into a smile and he put the chain around his neck. The pendant sat perfectly against the satin, the black background displaying it in all of its beauty.

'The city is in turmoil,' Eilean added. 'You will easily take it with an army this size. General MacMorna has gone south to bring his troops but will never get there in time to stop you. With the pendant the people will see you as the rightful leader of the realm.'

'Thank you for pointing that out,' replied Stealthman. 'That is exactly what I plan to do. Before I mobilise my army I would like to ask you one question.' He paused giving every one of them a lingering gaze before asking, 'Where is the tail?'

This is what they had dreaded. Leachim had mentioned that he might want the tail for himself to help complete his victory.

'We don't have it,' Fiona informed him. 'We brought the pendant to you and Leachim took the tail to the land of the faerie people. He said it was too valuable to be entrusted to us.'

Stealthman smiled at Fiona. 'You must be the clever one. Leachim said you had ability beyond your years. If you are so clever I should be wary of anything you tell me.'

'Why should you? It's true. Leachim would not let us take the tail with us on the journey home. He took it with him and he is probably in the faerie realm even as we speak.'

'I see,' he said, his eyes lingering on them. I would like you all to do me a great favour. I want you to try very hard, not to imagine the place where you are hiding the tail.' This strange request was difficult to do. Fiona immediately realised that Stealthman was reading their minds.

'Don't,' she screamed, trying to break the thoughts of the others. It was too late. He turned to his guards.

'You men! Search that wagon. There is a secret compartment under the floor.' Eilean grabbed for her sword as Heather reached for her bow when Stealthman's voice boomed.

'Leave the weapons. You would not last a minute.' It was true. They were in the middle of his camp and they would all have been killed. 'Besides,' he continued, 'I have no desire to see any harm come to you. You have humiliated Morbidea and that makes you an ally as far as I am concerned. Leachim knew he could never match my powers, which is why he made this deal with me. It has not worked for him as I never intended to keep my part of the bargain.'

The two guards approached and presented Stealthman with the

tail. He held it aloft with reverence and his eyes shone with the prospect of victory.

'And now the tail is also mine. Once I have taken the city, I will harness the power of the tail and, with the pendant also in my possession, there will be none to challenge me. Morbidea will be defeated forever,' cackled Stealthman.

Two men appeared from the marquee carrying an elongated metal box. Stealthman placed the tail inside and snapped the clasps shut.

'Put this in my treasure wagon and guard it with your life. I'm sorry you have gone to so much trouble, only to fail in the end but I'm sure you will still be relieved to be on your journey home. Think of the good you have achieved. Your faerie realm and your Earth are safe for the time being. Maybe someday in the future, if I feel like it, I shall bring my armies to visit you,' he turned, giving orders to break camp and returned to his marquee.

Fiona and the others took their wagon to a spot by the river with their spirit broken they mournfully set up camp for the night.

Chapter 31

THE LOST TAIL

The broken travellers sat round the fire. Their mood was sombre, each lost in their own thoughts. No one felt like talking or eating. They had achieved more than they ever imagined would have been possible. The odds had been against them and they had come through, only to have their prize taken from them at the last minute by a stupid mind trick. They had crossed the length and breadth of this cursed land, fighting against all the odds. They felt gutted and utterly defeated. Their worlds might be safe for the time being but

Stealthman's threat to visit them weighed heavily. How could things have come to this?

'We should follow them, watch them and wait for an opportunity to try and get it back,' Eilean said. Her outburst stemmed more from frustration than thinking. She didn't really believe they would have any chance of getting the tail a second time and she had no constructive idea of what to do next. The silence of the others only helped confirm this.

'We'll never get it back now. Stealthman won't let it out of his sight,' bemoaned Oxterguff staring dejectedly into the campfire. 'All we can do is return to the faerie queen and tell her what has unfolded. She may be able to make a suggestion as to what should happen next.'

'I'm going to clean up Meg,' announced Finn, getting up from the fire. 'The poor soul has been covered in all that dried mud since we left Sharagon's place.' He brought Meg over to stand in the heat and light of the fire and began to brush down her flanks. The dried mud fell away quite easily.

'Could you undo the ribbons from my tail,' asked Meg. 'They really are quite uncomfortable.'

'For goodness sake,' snapped Fiona, 'do you two not care what has happened? We have lost the tail. Our worlds are in danger and you two are having a grooming session.'

'That doesn't mean that Meg has to be uncomfortable,' replied Finn as he undid the rags woven into Meg's black tail.

'You can be so annoying sometimes, Finn,' snapped Fiona. Frustrated by failure, she left the fire and crossed to the wagon, hitting her clenched fist on the side. She wanted to cry but she was too angry.

'I'm sorry,' replied Finn, 'Maybe this will cheer you up.'

Fiona was furious. How could Finn possibly think anyone could be cheered up in this situation. She spun round to vent her full anger on her brother and what she saw stopped her in her tracks.

Finn was standing by the fire with the ribbons trailing to the ground in one hand. In his other was a silver-tooled handle with the grey tail shimmering in the firelight. Everyone looked up. There was a silence that seemed to last forever. They were all too stunned to speak. It was Finn himself who broke the silence.

'Well, you didn't think I was going to give Stealthman the real tail did you?'

Oxterguff was the first to respond. He jumped up screaming at the top of his voice and danced round the fire. 'He's been tricked, Stealthman's been tricked, Finn's got the tail and we've all been tricked.'

Finn was bombarded with questions as the excitement and relief poured from the ecstatic band of adventurers. There was much hugging, shouting and dancing about as it dawned on them they had succeeded in their quest. When the initial excitement passed, Finn settled them by the fire once more. They put a pile of logs on and as the sparks flew and the fire crackled, Finn explained to them what had happened.

'Leachim knew that he was not yet a great enough wizard to defeat Stealthman using only magic so he had to be very, very cunning. He knew that Stealthman would want the tail but he also knew of his ability to read people's minds. Without telling anyone, apart from me of course,' said Finn taking a bow, 'I gave the tail to Sharagon to make a replica using her transportation cabinets. Do you remember when Sharagon's servants, the Links, were smearing Meg with mud and dressing her down?' They all nodded and said they remembered. 'Well,' continued Finn, 'you'll remember that I went to help them weave the ribbons into her tail. It was then that I weaved the real tail into Meg's black tail and bound it round with the ribbons. The replica one came with us in the secret compartment of the wagon.

'That is genius,' laughed Oxterguff. 'Who would think of looking for a horse's tail on the back end of a horse?'

'Why do you think Meg was so quiet in Stealthman's camp. She didn't draw any attention to herself. No one, not even Stealthman noticed a horse yoked to a cart. He was so focussed on all of us and the picture in our minds that he didn't see the tail right under his nose.' Fiona smiled as she thought of Leachim. 'He really has worked this out so carefully. We were very lucky to have him on our side. We couldn't have done it without him. I'm surprised he trusted you though, Finn. You can never keep a secret.'

'I nearly told you, Fiona, but then I thought this is no ordinary secret. Also I had to wait until Stealthman and his soldiers were gone before I could tell you the truth. It was really hard to see you all so fed up and sad.'

'I think you've done remarkably well,' said Heather. 'Tomorrow we'll head home.'

That night they could not sleep for excitement. They rose early and after a quick breakfast prepared for the journey back. They decided to abandon the wagon as they felt they would be quicker on foot and did not want Meg burdened with the weight of it. Two days later they arrived back in the faerie realm and, when news of their success was heard, a great feast was planned.

To their utter joy they found that Leachim was with the faerie queen. The following day news came of great battles in the north. A war was raging but no one as yet knew who was winning.

In the afternoon everyone assembled in the amphitheatre by the well of the abyss. They gathered round as the queen reversed her spell that had turned Meg into an elegant black horse. Meg's body twitched and quivered as thousands of black butterflies fluttered from her leaving Meg a grey mare once more. The proof of their success was the fine grey tail swishing proudly behind her. The only other sign of their great achievement was the silver-tooled handle being held aloft by the queen.

As early evening approached the queen and Oxterguff travelled with their guests to the Yett. It was an emotional goodbye given all they had been through. Oxterguff shook hands with Finn then he graciously kissed the hands of Heather, Eilean and Fiona. He stroked Meg, patted Kirsty and gave a knowing nod to Mouldy who blinked his eyes back at him.

The queen stepped into the middle of the clearing. 'You have saved our worlds, my friends, and will forever be in our hearts. We have become allies in our fight against the evil that threatens our lands. It may be that we will one day require each other's help again. Until then we can close the Yett once more. We wish you well. Are you ready, my friends?' Fiona and Finn rushed forward and both gave Oxterguff a final hug.

'You take care, bairns,' he said, his voice breaking a little. They rejoined their group and the queen raised her hands. The journey back through the Yett began. They soared upwards through the waterfall, cascading rainbows of light dazzling their vision. Then they were there, once more at the top of the Grey Mare's Tail. Eilean was desperate to see her father and the children wanted to thank the laird. They descended to the caves beneath the waterfall. Their excitement was soon quashed when they found the caves deserted. The dwellings had been abandoned and there was no one to be seen. They made their way to check the stockade that had been the laird's dwelling but it too was deserted.

Emerging into the sunlight they were met by two handsome men. It took Finn and Fiona a moment to realise it was Wattie and Tam, the laird's guards. They informed them that the curse had been miraculously broken four nights before. Finn and the girls looked at one another, knowing it was exactly the same time the tail had been retrieved. The men were delighted to see Eilean and Heather safe and well.

'Come on,' cried Wattie, 'we know someone who will be ecstatic to see you.'

That evening another celebratory feast was held in the laird's castle. He was overjoyed to have his daughter and Heather back safe and well. As they celebrated, the laird filled them in on what had been happening. He explained that he had pardoned Callum and his friends and had even decided to forgive Paul for his betrayal. Paul, however, full of regret exiled himself. He had left the clan and disappeared. No one knew where he had gone. Eilean felt faintly glad of this as she did not know if she would ever have been able to forgive Paul. The following day it was time for another set of farewells.

'At least our friendships exist in this world,' said Eilean. 'We will hopefully see each other again.'

With the last of the farewells being said, Fiona and Finn, accompanied by Meg, Kirsty and Mouldy, set off for home. As they crossed the familiar landscape they came across the bully whose laces Finn had tied together. He was in exactly the same position. That was when the children remembered that time had been abandoned while they were gone. They continued on their journey in quiet. They had completed their task and saved their world from a terrible danger. Against all the odds they had won through. The truth of the matter was they were already missing the friends they had shared this amazing adventure with.

Arriving back at the farm, they went straight to the barn where the whole adventure had begun. It was quiet and still.

'Welcome home,' a familiar voice called from the corner.

'Leachim!' cried the children in unison.

'I was right about you, Fiona. You are, indeed, a remarkable girl. This quest would never have been accomplished without your wisdom and strength of character. You should be very proud of yourself. And as for you, Finn, there is more to you than meets the eye. You are a very brave young man. Until the next time.' Leachim slipped through the door of the barn and was gone.

Fiona put her arm around Finn. 'We had better go and see Mum,' she suggested. 'We'll have to be careful how we tell her things. She thinks we've just been in here doing our farm work.'

'I know,' Finn agreed. 'Fiona, things are never going to be the same again, are they?'

'No, Finn, they won't. Come on, let's go and see Mum.' She took his hand and they slipped through the barn door followed by Kirsty.

'Well, my friend,' hooted Mouldy, 'I don't know about you but I for one will be glad to have a bit of peace and quiet, for a wee while anyway.'

'You will not hear me arguing about that, old mate.' Mouldy took off up into the rafters and put his head under his wing. Meg swished her tail three times and settled into her stall.

And the bairns were right. Things never were the same again, as was very soon to be seen.

Garry Stewart is an award-winning actor, a writer and director who spends his time between Glasgow and his home in Andalusia. He was artistic director of Baldy Bane Theatre Company where he wrote and directed over 30 plays for children and young adults. He believes that humour and a clever animal or two are a great way to engage children in stories.

One of his early childhood memories was the excitement of waiting for the mobile library to arrive in the area of Edinburgh where he grew up. Climbing the huge steps to see the hundreds of books on the old wooden shelves that lined the large van, was where he discovered that stories could take you to places beyond the streets where you lived. *The Shanter Legacy* is Garry's first children's book.

TIPPERMUIR BOOKS

Tippermuir Books Ltd (est. 2009) is an independent publishing company based in Perth, Scotland.

PUBLISHING HISTORY

Spanish Thermopylae (2009)

Battleground Perthshire (2009)

Perth: Street by Street (2012)

Born in Perthshire (2012)

In Spain with Orwell (2013)

Trust (2014)

Perth: As Others Saw Us (2014)

Love All (2015)

A Chocolate Soldier (2016)

The Early Photographers of Perthshire (2016)

Taking Detective Novels Seriously: The Collected
Crime Reviews of Dorothy L Sayers (2017)

Walking with Ghosts (2017)

No Fair City: Dark Tales from Perth's Past (2017)

The Tale o the Wee Mowdie that wantit tae ken
wha keeched on his heid (2017)

Hunters: Wee Stories from the Crescent:
A Reminiscence of Perth's Hunter Crescent (2017)

A Little Book of Carol's (2018)

Flipstones (2018)

Perth: Scott's Fair City:
The Fair Maid of Perth & Sir Walter Scott –
A Celebration & Guided Tour (2018)

God, Hitler, and Lord Peter Wimsey: Selected Essays, Speeches and Articles by Dorothy L Sayers (2019)

Perth & Kinross: A Pocket Miscellany: A Companion for Visitors and Residents (2019)

The Piper of Tobruk: Pipe Major Robert Roy, MBE, DCM (2019)

The 'Gig Docter o Athole': Dr William Irvine & The Irvine Memorial Hospital (2019)

Afore the Highlands: The Jacobites in Perth, 1715–16 (2019)

'Where Sky and Summit Meet': Flight Over Perthshire – A History: Tales of Pilots, Airfields, Aeronautical Feats, & War (2019)

Diverted Traffic (2020)

Authentic Democracy: An Ethical Justification of Anarchism (2020)

'If Rivers Could Sing': A Scottish River Wildlife Journey. A Year in the Life of the River Devon as it flows through the Counties of Perthshire, Kinross-shire & Clackmannanshire (2020)

A Squatter o Bairnrhymes (2020)

In a Sma Room Songbook: From the Poems by William Soutar (2020)

The Nicht Afore Christmas: The much-loved yuletide tale in Scots (2020)

Ice Cold Blood (eBook, 2021)

Dying to Live: The Story of Covid's Sickest Patient (Grant and Amanda MacIntyre, 2021)

FORTHCOMING

The Perth Riverside Nursery & Beyond:
A Spirit of Enterprise and Improvement
(Elspeth Bruce and Pat Kerr, 2021)

Fatal Duty – The Scottish Police Force to 1952:
Cop killers, Killer Cops & More
(Gary Knight, 2021)

William Soutar: Collected Poetry, Volume I
(Published Work)
(Kirsteen McCue and Paul S Philippou (editors), 2021)

William Soutar: Collected Poetry, Volume II
(Unpublished Work)
(Kirsteen McCue and Paul S Philippou (editors), 2022)

Beyond the Swelkie:
A Collection of New Poems and Writings to Mark
the Centenary of George Mackay Brown (1921–1996)
(Jim Mackintosh & Paul S Philippou (editors), 2021)

A Scottish Wildlife Odyssey
(Keith Broomfield, 2021)

All Tippermuir Books titles are available from bookshops
and online booksellers. They can also be purchased directly
with free postage & packing [UK only].
(minimum charges for overseas delivery) from:
www.tippermuirbooks.co.uk

Tippermuir Books Ltd can be contacted at:
mail@tippermuirbooks.co.uk